Alien Trudge

Lead-Based Books

II

ISBN: 979-8-9908294-0-4 (Paperback)
ISBN: 979-8-9908294-1-1 (eBook)

Library of Congress Control Number: 2024912995

Any resemblance to persons living or dead is purely coincidental.

Front cover art by Billy Watson
Book design by Billy Watson

First printing edition

leadbasedbooks.com

Dedicated to my mother & father — the yin and yang of parenting. To Grandma and Uncle Micheal because without them, there would be no Alien Trudge. To my brother Alexavier, for providing copious amounts of inspiration. To my best friend and fellow alien Chase for being there always. To Mr. Morgan for serving as the catalyst for this book. And last but not least, to Miss Weight-of-the-World for showing me that there is intelligent life on this planet, and for also showing me there is always someone better.

CONTENTS

PREFACE

I don't know how I should start this, and I sure as hell don't know where. I suppose I'll start at the beginning: Here is where you can find my mind laid-out bear. These words which you are about to read are the scattered pieces of my soul – the blood from my heart which I ripped-out in order to write this book.

I started writing these vignettes and poems in the year 2020 – when I started high school – with no real intention of putting any of them into a book. The idea to write a book came a year later when a great man named John Morgan asked to see what it was I was writing in my notebook. I reluctantly put together a ten-page manuscript for him to read and upon seeing it, he asked if writing was the thing I wanted to do with my life. I said yes without hesitation, and he went on to give me the encouragement I needed to begin writing with purpose – that purpose being this book.

These stories and poems, these tender pieces of my soul which I lay before you are quite different from anything you've ever seen before. I say this not out of pompous arrogance; but from experience. Here, in this book, I take you through low times, high times, times of comedic pleasure, times of great stress; and much, much more. At some points you may laugh, at points you may cry, and by the end I might just make you feel ultimately angry.

And a word of caution: This anthology of alienation is not for the faint of heart. My words are harsh, this book is full of cursing. I tell tales of alien planets, filled with never-before seen scenes. Finding a publisher was hell, and I'm told that finding an audience will be even more difficult. I do not have the highest of hopes for this book, for hope is a fool's crutch, yet I put it out all the same.

Sometimes you may feel like you are drowning when in reality, you are just breathing. You may feel like Atlas as the world seemingly crushes you when the fact of the matter is you're only crushing yourself. This is the Alien Experience. Nobody understands and they never will but that's okay because you have yourself and that's enough – because you can always count on yourself to carry the weight of that pain.

CHAPTER 1:
Entering the Ten Chambers – Beginning of the End

The dark abyss shines so beautifully. It looks like a black diamond when it shimmers and gleams in the dim light of the forever fire of life. This abyss is only the very threshold of the Ten Chambers; the beginning of the end. The abyss calls out to me and wraps me up in its cold embrace when I come to it. Punks try to pull me out of the abyss so they can try and warm me up with their plastic heaters, but I evade them with ease as I sink deeper and deeper into my own complacency.

****

The Lowly Warrior stood amongst the lush field of green, knee-high grass and contemplated what it was he had to do. The line between life and death had at that point become so fine, yet still so well-defined. He knew the consequences, and they weighed heavily upon his shoulders. Had he come so far for nothing? Would he have walked such great distances and tread such perilous terrains just to give-up in the end? The answer would become clearer with time – or so the Lowly Warrior had hoped. As time passed and as the Lowly Warrior watched the grass sway in the gentle breeze, he figured that he would have to be like that grass – able to go with the flow of the wind, and yet never falling. So with that revelation, the Lowly Warrior unsheathed his saber and went forth with his ambitions. He knew that what he was about to do wouldn't be easy, and many would die in the crossfire; but fear had lost its grip on the Lowly Warrior as he began his Trudge in stride.

****

The ecosystem of this wasteland of a planet is unlike anything I have ever seen before. The temperature is 50 below freezing, yet everywhere I look there is foliage. The terrain is like a jungle, despite the sub-zero climate. The strange forest I find myself in is far more dangerous than even the most treacherous parts of the Amazon. The native species here is not unlike a human in its appearance, but their language and customs are completely incomprehensible to me. I hope to learn as much about their ways of life as I can – then perhaps Captain Ellsworth and I can terraform this planet and live here in peace.

****

I'm inside the Volcano
I'm not sure how or why

But this volcano is cold
It erupts snow instead of lava
I want to leave
But alas,
I have been forsaken to the Volcano
Never to leave
And so are you
****

All I can hear when they speak is mutant speech. The mall, gossipy rumors and bullshit, and that damnable social media crap. I question my own motives for being nice to any of them. A wise man once said, "I'm an alien man." I share that sentiment. I really shouldn't waste my time here on Earth; lingering in a pit of self-indulgent despair with the rest of these idiots.
****

It was in the great Black Void where I met her. Her depression entranced me and made me want her bad. Her sorrow and immense sadness was like a siren's call to me. I became a freak who admired her for her ability to roll with the punches and never complain about the pain. I fell selfishly in love with her eyes that spoke about suicide. I loved it when all she seemed to want to do was melt away into nothingness. I just wanted to drink it up; I yearned for a sip of her blues jam as if it were cognac and I were a rich alcoholic. I wanted her to talk volumes to me about how horrible she must have felt. I wanted to feel her bite me and break the flesh. All the hungry and healthy fish in the sea and I wanted the one who was full of shit and sick as a dog, typical.
****

The carnage was incredible
Many were ripped to shreds
Some may call it a calamity
I call it a devastation
I witnessed some go insane
I saw others smoke it away
A select few made it out intact
I'm one of those few

Class of 2024
****

I left them for dead
Don't rightly know if they survived
Probably died
Can't think about that now though
I have to keep traveling
My journey repeats everyday
The ocean
The tundra
Intermission in a cave
The forest
The jungle
The desert
And finally the Volcano
The isolation is only a little scary sometimes
It's like this everyday
Here in hell
We're all in hell
****

I don't know why I killed them. They were good enough people, I don't believe that they ever said anything bad about anyone. They never did steal and always gave to those in need. I suppose I was just jealous. I was jealous of how good they were and how the people always treated them with the utmost respect – while I was always treated like dirt. Jealousy and anger made me kill them. It wasn't a conscious decision. All I ever wanted was to be nice and respectable like them. So now they're dead, and I am God compared to their rotting corpses.
****

It had been a very long trudge for both Joe and Victoria. They were both tired beyond belief and in tremendous pain. The two eventually found respite atop a cliff so high above sea level that from the top, it seemed you could see the curvature of the world. The cliff overlooked the Atlantic Ocean and just over the horizon, you could see the sun starting its daily plunge into the water; resulting in the ocean reflecting a blinding, golden orange. There was a light breeze rolling off the ocean that evening. All at once, Joe became transfixed with Victoria's eyes, and Victoria with Joe's. The two embraced and wept tears of joy and relief as Victoria lit a match and threw it into the sea. Joe and Victoria turned their eyes back toward the sea – watching as the Atlantic became engulfed in flames. With the smell of napalm and burning flesh filling their noses, Victoria and Joe watched and smiled as the entire world burnt down before their very eyes.

****

I am married to a beautiful woman whom I never get to spend time with. Her name is Luna. Luna has a dim, silver glow to her skin. Her skin is so beautiful that it absorbs and reflects the very light around her. Luna has the power of a goddess. She controls all bodies of water on Earth with her ferocious spirit alone. Luna can move entire oceans without even touching a single drop of water.

My name is Helios. My skin glows so bright that it blinds all who stare at me. Like my wife, I too have god-like powers. I can move man and mud alike with my persuasive soul. In addition, I give plants the very energy they need to live. I somewhat covet my power, but I would steadfastly give it all up just to spend one moment with my precious Luna. But alas, that is not even a slight possibility and so all I can do is watch her from afar. Though I am always surrounded by admirers, I remain completely alone. I am truly the Lone Star.

****

Alone in this barren wasteland
Nobody, nothing, nowhere to go
I'm in purgatory
Hell doesn't want me
Heaven mocks me
All I want is to come back to life
But when I was alive
All I wanted to do was die
Maybe I should never have existed
Just another one of God's mistakes
Created to suffer

I am your savior
J.C.
****

They all died
I killed them
But wasn't it I,
Who gave them life in the first place?
I knew the consequences
But I didn't care
There was no carnage however
Upon death,
Flesh turned to dust
Leaving behind nothing but bone
Bone that has slipped deep into earth's many crevices
All life that I create is damned from the start
I often find myself getting bored
Their turmoil and dismay is my entertainment
****

Fuck my classic symbolism and allusion; I'm coming at you now with that raw and rugged realism, mixed with some cynical humor. It is so cold in here that even a polar bear would have to wear a jacket just to be comfortable. It's so cold that those who dwell in the fiery pits of hell, given the choice, would choose to stay where they are rather than trade me places. It's so cold that the US Government passed a law against such a temperature as this, deeming it cruel and unusual punishment. It is so cold, in fact, that the fire I lit put itself out with the bottle of water on the teacher's desk. It is so goddamn blood-freezing and mind-altering cold in this damnable place, that I have run out of jokes and am now going to freeze to death.
****

I still remember the fat cat from back in the day. The fat cat ate the rat. He walked into the parlor after hours, dressed in his pinstriped, black and gray suit. He sported his usual black velvet fedora with the gold studded brim, 24K gold watch, and two rings for each of his remaining nine fingers. The rat restlessly sat in the back, tied-up to a sturdy wooden chair that was chained to one of the steel pipes that ran up the wall. The cat walked quietly to the back and before eating the rat, he spoke to me some words which I will never forget. "Adal, my boy, there are pawts heeaw in da' first chamba – pawts that everyone must play in orda fo' da' world ta keep on spinnin'. Some people have da… unfortunate, pawt ta play of da' rat. The sad truth about our business heeaw, Adal, is that us cats must eat the rats in orda ta keep outa trouble from da' animal control, capish?" I nodded my head in agreement as the fat cat put two slugs into the rat's head. And with that, the rat is dead and the fat cat has been fed. Oh, and by the way, this is just some shit I made up on the fly. Merely some high school level biology.

****

Alone; I find myself becoming the definition of the word. I crave human interaction, and yet I hate humanity. I feel most alone in an overcrowded classroom full of people, so instead I choose to sit here in this vacant stairwell. No one is here but me, so I cannot possibly be alone. I am merely by myself. I cannot relate to any of these drug-fueled, phone addicted mutants. I hope to shine light on their darkness, but things are looking rather dim. I feel the solipsist rising in me as I begin to disregard everyone else's existence. Sometimes, I truly feel like the only real person in the world.

****

Literature my friend, why hath thou forsaken me so? Why did you exit the world so abruptly; leaving it in such utter chaos and dismay? The children of the world are starved for philosophy and poetry. The absence of the two has left a void in their souls, a void which they try to fill with memes and dark, cynical humor. But alas, with ignorance and blatant stupidity aplenty and running rampant, these substitutes are proving to be not nearly enough to fill the void. So now they are forced to turn to the literature of yester century. But the language proves to be too primitive, old words take on new and offensive meanings, and their overall messages have been lost on them. And it is at this point when I look into myself and find my true calling; to bring literature to my fellow ignorant children in a way that they will recognize and identify with.

****

Tonight's late-night soundtrack is Steely Dan. The track at this precise moment is Bad Sneakers; a beautiful and soulfully enriching tune that reminds me of long summer bike rides through the slums of South Bend. The sun starts its descent into the horizon as I navigate the desolate evening street on my chrome plated bike. My hatred and contempt for the futility of mortality fade away and all that remains is my love of the open road. As I ride farther and farther, and the sun descends lower and lower, the tune Midnight Cruiser comes to mind and I begin to feel like I am the midnight cruiser Jim Hodder once sang about. Time moves faster along than my wheels can roll me and before I know it, the stars are out in the sky; but I still do not feel a great need to return home. People often ask me why I enjoy riding so far from home. I can never satisfy their question with a precise answer, because in order to understand what it is like to be twenty miles from your home with only your BMX bike to get you back and some chump change to buy a drink, you really have to experience it for yourself. Riding is the only way for me to deal with this middle-class drag of a life. But then again, I suppose your way of smoking, shooting, and drinking it all away is perfectly reasonable too.

****

She looks at me with absolutely no pity or hesitation and shoots me directly in my right foot. As I trip and begin to fall from the pain, she catches me and shakes me by my neck; screaming, "You made me do this!". She does this for a good thirty seconds before dropping me on the hardwood floor and walks into the back room behind her. She reemerges a full ten minutes later holding my best friend's severed head in her right hand and a 28 inch long machete in her left. She vigorously shakes the head in front of my face and yells, "This is all your fault! You were supposed to look out for him, you two were brothers! But instead you let him fuck around with dirt like me and now he's dead and you're all alone on this alien planet!" She then throws the head behind her back, and it makes a loud thump as it cracks the drywall behind her. She climbs on top of my weak from blood loss body, cuts my tongue out, and finally, she severs my head to add to her collection.

****

She slithers through the ten chambers, sneaky and quiet as a New York cat burglar. She'll bite you, you know. She will sink her small and easily hidden fangs into your neck and release into your bloodstream her semi-deadly hallucinogenic poison. Of course, while you writhe and squirm in pain there on the ground like a slug in salt, she'll use her kung fu to cripple you beyond escaping. This will be the moment when the hallucinogen will kick-in and you will mistake your fear of lonely painful death for true love. So now that you're so "in love" with this evil woman, you decide to marry her – playing directly into her plot. The poison's effects are so strong that you don't even realize what it is you are engaged to. That's no woman! That right there is a Killer Kung Fu Wolf Bitch!

****

Often I look unto humanity and all I can see is trash and scumbaggery. I see how those canine men out there act in their desperation for sexual intercourse, and it makes me feel ashamed to be a man. I recently learned of this reptile called the whiptail lizard. This particular animal reproduces asexually, meaning they have no use for sex. Many of my thoughts lately have been of what humanity would be without the constant distraction that is the lust for sex. I look upon these whiptail lizards and I feel that they are the most logical evolutionary step (despite evolution typically going in the reverse direction). Fuck genetic diversity, there are enough diverse characters on this mudball to fill a million unique zoos.

****

Am I going too fast for you? Am I rocking too hard? Is it possible that I of all people am weighting too hard for you? Is my stomp too loud? Is my disposition too hateful for you to handle? Is it possible that my mere glance alone has completely dissected you and left you with no self respect at all? You keep freezing up in my presence so what the hell is it? Do you view me as so much of a scumbag that I don't deserve to be treated like a normal human being? Did you take all my jokes seriously? Do you think that since they flirt with me in the stairwells, that I've screwed a couple of them? Am I perceived as sexist because of my low opinion of most teenage girls? Can you imagine me sucking on a bottle of Jack & Daniel's, or gripping a needle? Is your view of me and my world that twisted? Damnit, I'm done talking to you – I can't imagine why I ever started in the first place.

INTERMISSION 1:

SUPER JESUS I

He's going faster and harder than any human to have ever lived. He is the one and only, Super Jesus! He can bite through diamonds like they're chocolate chip cookies. He can bend steel rods between his fingers like they're clay. He can fly and even shoot a laser out of each eye, he's incredible! Super Jesus can walk on water and lava too! He was crucified twice, that's why he's the ultimate Christ!

Girls don't like Super Jesus because they say he's too much of an egotistical, judgemental, narcissist; so whenever he's horny, Super Jesus drugs and rapes whoever he pleases. One time, when there were no fine pieces of ass in his general vicinity, SJ became so overwhelmed with sexual desire that he jerked off in a bed of flowers in a public park. His divine semen mixed with the flowers, mutating their offspring and creating demigod plant creatures, who ascended to heaven and have since ruled over all plant life on Earth. There was another time, similar to this one, when SJ fucked a racoon and created Racoon Jesus.

One time, the pigs tried to kill Super Jesus with their puny little guns. Little did they know, Super Jesus is impervious to everything that isn't crucifixion. The bullets ricocheted off Super Jesus' lean and toned body and shot right back through the pig fuckers who tried to kill him.

I once had the honor of meeting the Ultimate Christ. It was a hot day out in the Arabian desert. I was about half a click from my mud hut, just taking my routine evening stroll, when there was a sudden flash of blue light. Back in Black by ACDC began playing as Super Jesus descended from the heavens above. He looked at me with those big brown eyes of his and asked in his raspy, deep voice, "Yo nigga, got any smokes on you?". I just so happened to have a fresh pack of menthol Newports on me, so I opened it up and held it out toward my savior. Super Jesus smiled at me, revealing his perfectly crooked and orange colored teeth, as he took the whole pack and said, "Good looks young blood.", before ascending back to the heavens. Long live the King of the King of Kings – long motherfuckin' live Super Jesus!

CHAPTER 2:
Thicker Mud

A thought just occurred to me the other day. I have been playing the "demo" version of life for quite some time now, and very soon, I will have to pay the price and get the full version. Just in case my metaphor is lost on you, I am saying that I will soon be an adult. It's funny, you know, how one minute you're on the kitchen floor playing with toy trucks and cars and then the next, you're graduating high school and trying to figure out what the hell a W-2 is. I fear the nine to five, the fat wife and the ungrateful brats who always seem to need something expensive. I fear the shiftless living graveyard that is middle class living. Life in the middle class is really too stressful, too meaningless, boring, and tiresome for my tastes to tell you the truth. I prefer a life of endless shifts and adventures. I strive for the unnatural, the unheard of, the spectacularly bombastic life of someone who doesn't just sit back and let society catch you in its jaws. So I suppose that rather than trying to hold onto these easy years, I should give them a grateful farewell as I begin my adventure into a whole new chamber.

****

It's late at night when I start to wonder to myself, what if this has all happened before? What if I'm one spec moving from timeline to timeline, just trying to get it right? Have we all lived multiple lifetimes, or is time simply on repeat? Sometimes I truly believe in the latter. It feels like we're all just moving through the phases of the universe sometimes. And that thought too raises even more questions in my mind. Is everything that ever will and ever has happened just part of some story being told over and over again? Are all my efforts toward a better life futile? I don't know, but I must not dwell on theories and conspiracies. These are thoughts that have trapped a many a man into a situation that he cannot possibly escape. I must be ever flowing like water in an untouched stream. I must be light that bends and reflects in any way it can just to continue forward.

****

Throughout the vast openness of reality that seems so endless, only one being truly and ultimately exists. One mind that creates illusions in order to satisfy its own thirst for amity in the lonely void which it resides in. Time and time again the mind has attempted to create the perfect false reality and time and time again, the universe has been imperfect. All of what you know is fake. But how can anything be fake when everything is fake? All this trash that passes for music nowadays; how could it possibly exist in a timeline blessed enough to hear the immaculate melodies of John Coltrane? America makes absolutely no sense either. Our political system, for instance, is a joke. Red or blue? It doesn't matter, both sides will ultimately disappoint you. How can you believe in a universe so improbable, so grim? I fully support the destruction of this faux world. Your so-called life means absolutely nothing; run rampant with this and do whatever you please. Hug the ones you love, kill the ones you hate. Rape and theivery, it's what funds your media outlets. Drugs and unclimbable ladders, it's what powers your economy.

****

Cold, the world describes a painful temperature. The cold bites through your flesh; it will hurt your very bones. It slows your brain. The heat given off by the sun is the exact opposite. The sun heals you with what Rollins would call "soul intensity". Many civilizations have worshiped the sun over the centuries, a well-known example being the Ancient Egyptians. They knew the sun as an almighty God that ruled over all of creation. The sun even absorbed other Gods within their own religion: such as Amen-Ra (once Amon and Ra), and Ra-Harakht (once Horus and Ra).

****

Waiting for warmth
Waiting for relief
Waiting for you
The cold is suffocating me
My last breath draws closer and closer
I keep waiting on death
But you never come
Perhaps I am already in hell
A hell with icy tundras
Instead of fiery caverns
So I suppose

I must conclude
I am waiting for the end of time
****

Sometimes I feel like I am on a conveyor belt. I feel like another middle-class dipshit teenager turning down all of his opportunities in life, in favor of a "stable" and "secure" life. Fuck that shit man. I don't want to live in a midwest city I hate all my life, just to end up dying in this miserable cold. Every passing second brings me just that much closer to my inevitable death, and it's pissing me off. All I want to do is destroy the world at times like this. I hate dealing with all these sellouts, scumbags, and braindead mutants. I hate being compared to family members who are going off to college with absolutely no clue what they even want to do in life. My mother says that I'm too much like my father. I guess it can't be helped. Are you laughing at me right now? Thinking to yourself, "I remember being like that when I was younger."? That's alright, it's just a phase. My hunger for a better life will wear off and I'll join you in that middle-class hell soon enough.
****

I am a nomad on this planet. I move from place to place, never settling down in one spot for too long. You can catch me in the west stairwell, where you tried to light your shit and smoke it. You can see me in the east stairwell, where you tried to fuck your boyfriend. One of your girlfriends will eventually try to flirt with me in the main stairwell, and that's when I decide to go to class.

All of this really drains me of my patience. I'm starting to truly despise school; where I once enjoyed to go and learn and read. I used to think, back in grade school, that I might one day in high school have a girlfriend. But now, seeing how girls my age act, I stay far away from them. There are no intelligent females that I have ever met in this place. They all seem to either be merely brainless, on drugs, criminals, or all three. I used to like the idea of having someone to confide to, but now I don't like the idea of any of these animals knowing anything about me.
****

Today I will die, yet again. Dying is such a funny process. Everything just goes black for what feels like an eternity. Then there's a flash of blinding light and you're in the endless white and gray speckled void. The static is deafening and the movement you will experience would have made you vomit in life. Without a sense of what is up or down in the void, you will not know if you are rapidly falling or rising, but you will be moving. As you approach the bottom or top, an overwhelming wave of blistering hot air will hit you like a tidal wave as the smell of sulfur fills your nostrils. The white and gray void turns red and you realize that there is no heaven, only hell. You stand in complete awe before Satan himself. He is no less than twenty feet tall, with the head of a king cobra and a crimson colored lion's mane around his neck. This anthropomorphic creature wears a suit befitting Iceberg Slim himself. A red pinstripe overcoat and matching pants with gold stitching, complete with a midnight black shirt and tie. Satan tells you in his wispy high-pitched voice which sector of hell you have been damned to. Occasionally, he will sentence a truly despicable soul to life on Earth. I am one of those souls. Everytime I die, he sends me back to Earth to live out yet another lifetime of dull mortal activity. Like Danzig, I am tired of being alive. I would much rather be in hell for eternity than toil around this mudball for any longer.

****

I despise teenagers. All they ever do is text on chatsnap, talk gossipy bullshit, and fight. Oh yes, they also do drugs. Some days it feels like I can't turn a corner in my school without someone hastily stuffing their weed-filled vape into their pocket, thinking that I am a security guard or a teacher. Whenever I hear someone talk about how "different" or "revolutionary" my generation is, I scoff. They smoke the same shit as their parents, the only difference is nobody gives a shit anymore. They all think that all that the weed they smoke is some sophisticated passtime because of its portrayal in the media. All those lyrics about how it enhances creativity, they must think that they are young Picassos. I can't really blame the messenger though, you might know what I mean.

****

The bastard eyes of a predator
When meat hangs mere inches in front of them
So close

But no touchy
You're too good for that!
But the meat,
It's practically calling out to the predator
"Please come eat me!"
The meat begs to be eaten
This makes the predator yearn even more
The predator decides to eat the meat
Afterwards
The predator feels like dirt
Now it's just like daddy
The predator slits its own throat
****

Dear Anonymous,

      I do not know your name, but I deeply appreciate you killing me. The gratitude I feel toward you is immeasurable. Now that I am dead, I have been able to find out the reason behind the universe's existence; there is none. Everything happens at random with absolutely no pattern, no algorithm. There is no fate, no soul mates; it's all just a big ass scam. But now that I'm dead, I don't really give a fuck. I cannot and thus will not tell you exactly what it is like to be dead, nor can I tell you what lies on this side of existence. I will, however, tell you that you and everyone else back on Earth are in for quite a treat.

Yours Truly,
    Joe C.
****

Everyday is an open opportunity
Every second poses a new risk
Any action may lead to disaster
False or correct?
You won't know until it's too late
One step may lead to devastation
Your undoing is inevitable

****

Good music is like poetry. Music has, afterall, been used to accompany poems for centuries. Even music without lyrics can be poetic. I can hear the emotional words of remorse coming from Coltrane's saxophone whenever I hear Naima. I wish I could create such amazing poetry such as that but alas, I have no talent, no musical ability whatsoever.

****

Most of my peers seem to dislike me at best. And looking at myself from their perspective, I can see why. My overall disposition can be a bummer at times. I can be too analytical and I can see why that would get on some people's nerves. Sometimes people just want to sit down, play on their phone, and mellow out to brainless music whose lyrics make no sense. Who am I to tell them why I don't think that's an acceptable way to spend eighty percent of their time? I mean, I'm sure you wouldn't like it if I told you to cut the bullshit and actually make something out of your life! That would be absurd.

****

Brainless apes
You thought normal apes were stupid?
How about these youths?
Monkey noises
Dog noises
They exuberate brain rot
They are just normal teenagers though
So I must face reality
I'm the invasive species
Might as well destroy their ecosystem
Since I'm here

****

Sometimes passing mutants in the stairwell peer into my notebook as I write. Their brains cannot possibly comprehend why someone would rather spend time writing in a book, than to spend it fucking or vaping; or doing both at the same time. If they tried to read some of the things I write in this book, I do not think that they would believe I am truly the same age as them. I know that I shouldn't be so hard on my peers though. It's truly not their fault that there is not any modern literature to stimulate their minds. Our English teachers are only getting older, and the way they teach doesn't suit the majority of students. So my words have become my own language, and they don't speak it.

****

Human interaction
I hate your version of it
I only want to experience it my way
Like when someone asks what you're reading
You respond "In Cold Blood"
And then they walk away
That's just how I like it

****

You can get used to used to the pain of being stabbed. You can go with the flow of the poison tide. No matter what, you will still eventually die. This may make it seem futile to avoid the knife when it comes for your throat, or to swim against the poison tide. But even though these are the more difficult options, you should go for them. Don't conform to who they want you to be and how they tell you to act. Be your own person. This may sound generic, but I feel that this is an important lesson in today's society of constant social media influence. So what if the newest jackass on Instagram says that being down with whatever it is you like isn't cool anymore? Fuck cool. Burn the mask, stomp its ashes into the pavement and show them all how it really is. Why should you have to keep putting up with these peons who spit in your face and mock you everyday? No matter how good you make yourself look for their sakes, you're still going six feet deep one day anyway. So you might as well go out on your own terms. Do you really think that following their ideas and their trends for the rest of your young life will really make you happy? Don't stay on this simple path that they paved for you. Go out and carve your own.

****

Sometimes I get into these dramatic fits of loneliness. Even as an adolescent, I am starting to realize the full extent of life's toll on my mind. I look into the future and the way that things are now, assuming everything continues on as planned, I see no wife or kids. To be honest, I am relieved. I am completely terrified of the thought of becoming a family man in the future. I'm so young and yet this cold path can already prove to be trying at times, as is the case with Miss Weight-of-the-World. You'll likely read something by her or see a work of art created by her in the coming years, but I won't write her name and jinx it. She's irresistibly intelligent and beautiful – thankfully she has high ambitions and no time for anyone but herself.

****

Roses are red

Violets are blue

I'd like to murder you

Hang you from the rafters

Put you out like a light

Please submit to me your body

Surrender your soul

Surrender your life

There will be no more pain

No more strife

…

Well I didn't want you that bad anyway

Your soul is probably stale

Your body is too weak for my needs

Your life has been infected

You need to be dissected

****

It was brutal. Blood and guts spattered everywhere, the hallway ended up looking like a scene from a Rob Zombie movie. It was an average day when he walked up to me. Without speaking a word, he pulls a .44 caliber handgun from his backpack. The sick mother put the gun to his head and all I can do in that moment is stare at him like a deer in headlights. We both stood there, staring blankly into each others' eyes

for what felt like hours. As time progressed, and as I looked even deeper into his eyes, fear turned to lust. I wanted in that instant, and I wanted him bad. My need to have him transcended physical means, it far surpassed all logical, emotional, and mental limitations. The need to have him inside me was a mere molecule compared to my need to be inside of his world – a main character in his story. Then in an instant he whips the gun around and shoots me twice in the chest, once in the head. As a disembodied soul on my way to hell, I watched as he ran to my corpse and started to undress me. Nowadays I spend all my time just waiting, waiting for my newfound love to join me down here in hell.
****

I once asked him why it is that he never had any regard for his or anyone else's life. It was a magnificent summer evening. We sat atop a tall cliff that overlooked the ocean. The sun had begun its descent into the horizon and its orange light shown across the water, making the sea look as if it was filled with liquid bronze. Light from this gorgeous sunset reflected off his brown eyes that looked red at that moment as he told me, "We all end up dying one day anyway, so why bother wasting what fleeting energy we have actually caring about anything?" I pointed out the hypocrisy in his philosophy by asking "But why bother conserving the energy normally used to care if you don't even acknowledge that very energy as important?" He smiled warmly at me and responded, "That is our greatest paradox." He kissed me on the cheek for the last time and proceeded to pull a handgun from the inside pocket of his jacket. He put the barrel inside of his mouth and pulled the trigger as the sun became fully submerged in the ocean. He may have had a bleak and pessimistic view on life, but he was sure to make his death somehow beautiful and sanguine.
****

I walked the endless hall of time. All of the sudden I was sideways. I witnessed a guy rip his lungs out and fry them. I had to tell myself it was normal. I jumped off of a ledge and took flight. The elephants were huge, as tall as a structure I had a faint memory of. Wide as a blue and green mass I'd seen once, I believed it to be called Earth. I couldn't remember who I was or where I was, or how I got there for that

matter. It mattered not now. I fell onto the ground, now taller than the elephants. I could see everything from that high up. All of the sudden I was small as a strong picnic creature. There was a giant shoe in the sky. It was headed for me. Now I was on fire, the smell of burning flesh was strong in my nose. A giant demonic creature came and picked me up, and ate me. I woke-up. All of my memories came back at once. I remembered the Eiffel tower, I remembered the ants. I was in a hospital with doctors and scientists surrounding me, I was chained to the bed. "We temporarily killed you.", said a scientist on the right of me, closest to my head. "In case your memory hasn't fully returned, your name is Bob Joe and you raped and dismembered over fifty children. They were all between the ages of five and thirteen. You're worse than John Wayne Gacey, you son of a bitch!" "Ok, that's enough Todd." said another scientist at my feet. "We killed you temporarily in order to know what hell looks like. So tell us, how would you describe your experience?" I could only think of two words to describe hell and they were, "Distorted Reality."
****

These braindead oafs worship their precious little football. They drive and fly here, South Bend, Indiana, from all over the damn place, just so that they can see some burly men with overcompensation issues chase a misshapen ball around a field. They get high and drunk off their fat asses and participate in their little American style Sabbath at Notre Dame. When I ride past on my bike, all I can do is stare in disgust and bewilderment. Then all they can do is stare back at me with that stick-up-the-ass look that all Notre Dame diehards seem to have. They're all just road poison. Fuck your little pigskin and by association, fuck you.
****

I like the weirdos, you know the kind. The kind on the streets, the ones with nothing left of their souls. They're usually drunk, high, crazy, or a combination of all three; it doesn't matter which. I like them all, and they all seem to love me. The weirdos stop me as I ride my bike so they may conversate. Most of what they say is uninteresting drivel, but it is good fun to see them treat me like an old friend. "Remember those homeless white folks from Blank Street?" one may spew, "I think you might be my nephew! Do you know Danielle?" another might ask. Funny shit right? I almost always answer their inquisitions with bullshit answers so I may become amused. "Oh yeah, I remember those old white folks!" "Hmm, yeah, I think I know someone named Danielle." I used to be afraid of strangers when I was a little kid, but now I adore them. I adore screwing with them anyway.

****

First, they nail me to a wall and watch me squirm. Next, they take me down and beat me with wooden bats and steel crowbars until I pass-out. Once I wake-up, I'm in a pig pen, surrounded by pigs feasting on slop. Then I'm shoved into a small, pitch-black room for a couple of hours. Once they've decided that I have had enough of that, they throw me to the mutants and force me to try and communicate with them. Proceeding that, they strip me of my tattered rags that I call clothing, nail me to a table, and perform all sorts of biological experiments on my body. Finally, when all is said and done, I receive my ultimate reward; a shot in the head by a handgun. They leave my corpse in the death room at night so I can recharge and go through the same thing again tomorrow.

****

The following goes out to all of you chickenshit, gun-toting assholes out there who bring their little guns to school, calling themselves the man:

So, you think that you're really some kind of macho-man with that little machine on your hip, don't you? You think the guys will respect you as long as you have that little peashooter, hotshot? Well motherfucker, do you think the girls won't notice that your cock is only four inches long? Are you even going to use your little "strap"? Oh, you are? Well then shoot me you scared sonofabitch. Cock back, put the barrel to my skull, and prove that you can't fight for shit. If you really are the shit, prove it by killing me in front of the pigs. Imagine being so lightweight, so weak, that you have to wear a gun on your hip, not unlike some wild western cowboy, just to prove your own self worth. How pathetic.

INTERMISSION 2:

TRUE TALES OF ADOLESCENCE PT. 1

A couple of years ago I, at the tender age of ten, was offered the services of a prostitute. At the time, I just barely had an inkling of an idea of what sex even was. My buddies had been the ones to tell me what it was, but I had no interest in trying it out for myself. Looking back on those days, it is in fact a miracle that I, a somewhat gullible and naive kid, did not fall victim to the drugs and sex I exposed myself to. Perhaps it was the result of good parenting, or maybe I was always a square at heart – who knows.

Back then I had a few good friends in the neighborhood. One of my buddies (whom I'll call Jerome) and I were especially close. Jerome was about five feet and three inches tall, just two inches taller than I was at the time. He had long dreads down to his shoulders and skin like dark chocolate. Jerome was a grade ahead of me, but we never let that get in between our friendship. We would often hang out at the park, or just ride our bikes endlessly through the neighborhood; all the while getting into all sorts of shenanigans. Back then, I thought that Jerome and I would be friends forever. We often dreamt of opening our own mechanic shop for cars and bikes when we grew up. Sadly though, Jerome and I grew far apart as we got older, and so it has been over four years since we last truly hung out.

Anyway, Jerome had an uncle who I'll call Jamie who was on house arrest, only a street over from Jerome's place. The guy wasn't exactly insane, but he had been systematically brainwashed into acting like a young fool, despite him being in his mid thirties. Jerome's uncle Jamie had always scared the crap out of me. He once pulled out a loaded handgun and started playing around with it, treating it like a toy gun. If I got caught up in a situation like that nowadays, I would calmly make an excuse to leave and then get the hell out of there. But at age ten, I was a bit hard headed and desperate for friends my age. I also had a knack for getting myself into dangerous situations. So anytime Jerome suggested that we go over to Jamie's house, I would tag along.

Almost every time I was over there, there was this tall, blonde woman walking around the house. I remember the woman being about six feet tall. She had long, blonde, curly hair and her skin had a yellow glow to it. I don't remember anything in particular about her face, but I do remember that she had the biggest breasts I had ever seen, a visually appealing ass, and long, slender legs. Every remaining memory I have of her is of her wearing a white, skin tight crop top with pink lettering on it that read, "Pussy is the most expensive food you'll ever eat". I couldn't for the life of me figure out what that meant. I knew by this time that pussy is slang for vagina, I just couldn't understand for the life of me understand why anyone would want to eat one; let alone pay to eat it. Anytime I saw her, she was only wearing that crop top and a pair of pink panties. I remember just staring at her whenever I saw her. Not only was she one of the most objectively attractive women I had ever seen up to that point, but I had also never seen a real live woman wearing only her underwear before.

One day, as I stared in awe at the woman, who walked straight down the hall perpendicular to the couch I was sitting on, a man who I had never noticed before came over to me. I did not know it at the time, but the man was a very low level pimp, probably with just one woman in his stable. He wore acid washed bluejeans, sagged passed his ass, and a white wife beater. He was nothing like the pimps you might read about in one of Iceberg Slim's books. Not even his hair resembled that of a stereotypical pimp, seeing as he sported a shag cut with a fade.

The nothing pimp stood before me in his full five foot nine glory and asked, "You ever fucked a bitch before, young blood?" Of course, I truthfully told him no. I was intimidated by his presence and the idea of lying had not even occurred to me. He put on a mask of fabricated shock (which I mistook for genuine shock at the time, leading to other overconfident adventures in the future) and exclaimed, "Really? You a virgin for real?" I had never even heard the word virgin up to that point, but given the context I became 85 percent sure of what he meant and nodded my head yes.

The guy plops himself down on the couch beside me and asks in a cunning voice, "How would you like to fuck that white bitch over there?" He points down the hall at an agape bedroom door where the tall blonde woman was sitting on top of a dirty old mattress. The woman didn't even look up when her body was offered to someone who was very clearly a minor. The thing that shocked me the most back then, however, was that she didn't at all refuse to have sex right there and then.

I turned down the almost tempting offer, being too shy to just on the spot have sex with some stranger whose name I didn't even know. My lack of a sex drive also helped me choose the right choice and "just say no" as Satan's wife would have said. The pimp was shocked, this time for real. "Damn, you serious?" exclaimed the Too Short wannabe. I sat in nervous silence as he continued, "So you just not ready, huh?" Taking my chance to get out of a possibly bad situation, I frantically nodded my head and the pimp continued his spiel, "Well, if you ever want some pussy just hit me up." He stands up and continues, "Yep, just call on Uncle Joe!" (I can't remember his full name, but I distinctly remember him calling himself Uncle 'Something'.) It was just that old, "You can trust me brother! We're both black, that makes us family!" routine.

I reflect on this memory with a smile on my face; just thinking about how oblivious to the world I was only a couple of years ago. Throughout the multiple drafts of this chapter, this story has begun to feel more and more like another lifetime. Now of course, you may be inclined to ask, "Would you have taken the pimp's offer now that you're a hormone-infested teenager?" Well, I'll answer your hypothetical question with blunt honesty. Knowing what I know now, despite being a stupid teenager, I would still refuse an offer of sex with a strange woman. Strange women scare me; and usually have a few STDs.

CHAPTER 3:
Enveloped in the Literature Blues

You can never truly prepare for anything. You will always be unprepared, underdressed; you can't know exactly what's going to happen next. You can go ahead and try to prepare for the most expected outcome, but life will throw you that ever so elusive curveball. That I promise.

…

Sometimes I feel less like an alien and more like a monster. My animalistic tendencies make me feel like I belong in the jungle. All I feel when I'm around the humans at school is sadness and hatred. I won't write here what I want to do when I'm surrounded by all those people, you would only laugh.
****

"Would you still love me if I proved myself to be insane?" Those were his last words to Jeniffer before he pushed her down the stairs at school. He thought she was obsessed. Jeniffer never seemed to give him any time to be alone with his thoughts. He loved the way Jeniffer would hurt him though. The way she bit into his flesh when they fucked, the way she would slash his arms open and pour lemon juice in the wounds. She was truly spectacular. All that masochistic shit was the bomb, but he just didn't think Jeniffer's over-attachment was worth it. The guy ended-up hanging himself a week after pushing Jennifer, because it was only after she was gone that he realized she was the only one for him.
****

Bullshit and perfume
When they pass me by
I smell only perfume
But when they stop and talk
I smell bullshit
They aren't good liars
Wolves in sheep's clothing
Devils dressed in white
Sirens singing their song
Just another ticket to the 9 to 5
Hahahaha
No thank you

****

My Pacon Blues; they're with me always. I crave human interaction with someone who won't just end up making me feel like an alien. I need bloodshed above all else though. I'm a fiend for carnage and action. When the time comes, when the clock ticks for the final time, I'll be angry. I'll wonder why I never did a damn thing with my life. I'll wonder why I took so much shit from all these fake fucks. Even now, I wonder why I am the way I am. I have self respect; that is to say I have absolutely no respect for anyone who I feel is not at least living up to my own standards. I hate my own generation because of this, but what has caused me to think this way? Why can't I tell my mother all these things I keep meaning to tell her? I'm afraid to stop writing. I don't want to face outward right now, I might break out in tears if I do. I just want to wrap my arms around myself and wither away.

****

These girls take all this trivial high school shit so serious. I can't understand why guys my age date them. Shit, if I did date, I would want to go for a full-grown woman; no younger than 27. In my school, when some cute guy talks to one of these homely country chicks, or when some jackass hipster starts some new trend on ChatSnap, the girls talk about it like politics. So shallow and vain are they all.

...

The alien blueprint, my anatomy. I don't relate to any of these people at all. I'm such a narcissist that I'm beginning to hate their mere constant babbling. I was unable to focus on the literature, so I popped in the earbuds and started writing this funky shit. These people are so brainless and obnoxious. At times like this, I really want to return home. I want the mothership to come pick me up so I can join Coltrane, Lynott, Miller, and all the other aliens who have graced humanity with their presence. I used to think that I could befriend some of them – fuck that shit.

****

Some of these mutants are hilariously self righteous. Earlier today one of them and its friends walked into class, laughing hysterically. When asked what was so funny, the leader mutant responded, "We were

just bullying someone out in the hallway." What type of shit is that? I said nothing, but thankfully someone else shared my own sentiments and told the leader that what she did was past unfunny. How can you be so fucked in the head, that you purposely make someone else feel like shit, and then laugh about it as if fucking Dave Chapelle himself was out in the hallway making jokes? That particular mutant is probably just insecure about her weight. I suppose it would be hard to face the day being a candidate for My Six Hundred Pound Life, especially with all these brain-dead anorexic girls walking around. Her fat ass won't get any sympathy from me, however. She probably feels the need to knock others down a few pegs, so that she may feel just a little better about herself. This is a prime example of yet another reason why I have no respect for my so-called peers. They don't even have any respect for themselves.
****

"Spilling Over the Side" by Rollins Band. I'm lonely, it's November, what else is new? These literature blues are getting pathetic. I'm not sure which is worse; the loneliness or the realization that everyone around me is fucking insane.

...

Men who get married become weak. They become dependent upon their woman. They need their wives to cook for them, to clean, to take care of the kids – you already know. Me personally, I don't need another mother. It gets even more pathetic when the woman decides that she's had enough, and up and leaves the poor sucker. The man will typically turn into this overweight pile of watery mud (with few exceptions). The pile of overweight mud will do damn near anything to convince the woman to come back; but to no avail. Even my own classmates, whose relationships are all built on lies anyway, seem to just fall apart when their girlfriends leave them. Even sometimes when it starts to hurt a little, I know I am winning because I'm not a pathetic pile of mud; I am an immaculate statue carved out of bronze.
****

I'm feeling really fucked up right now. I feel like I'm dying. I want to scream. I'm real tired man, tired of this winter bullshit. I'm so exhausted from the seemingly endless months of this midwest winter. I

don't even feel like this is my life anymore. I'm not the one calling the shots anymore. I am just a well programmed automaton. Work work work and nothing else matters. Today is going to be even more hellish than yesterday if this literature blues shit continues. It's past midnight and I don't give a fuck. Sleep is a recurrence I wish I could live without. All I seem to have is nightmare after nightmare anyway so fuck it. My throat hurts from all the silent screaming I do all day long. I can't possibly face the hellhole in the morning. I might just break down, like some machine. This is my self destruction; I'm going out with a bang.
****

It was already a shit day for Jim. I could tell that something was wrong when I saw him fidgeting in his seat. As soon as Mrs. Calahoochi walked in, she immediately began tearing into him. Something that I had noticed about Jim was his impeccable ability to take abuse, without retaliating. On this particular day, however, he had a certain aura of doom surrounding him. After a full minute of verbal abuse from Mrs. Calahackit, Jim got up out of his chair. He pulls a gun out of his pants and says his final words, "Hope you enjoy the look of blood spatter covering your walls, you raging bitch." Jim put the barrel of the gun to his right temple and pulled the trigger. Blood spattered the walls. Mixed in with the blood are pieces of Jim's skull, flesh, and brain matter. Mrs. Calahasse looks over Jim's corpse with disgust as she drags him out into the hallway. When she reenters the room, Mrs. Calzone begins the day's lesson – as if nothing of importance had just happened.
****

Humans are just fancy animals. **HEY** We do not love, we all just hate each other deep down. Our brains are hardwired to fuck and that's all there is to it. **GET OUT** But we always go and complicate everything anyway. We lie to each other and ourselves. Fearful of the lonely grave, we marry someone we'll either leave or drive away. **OF MY** In our selfish need for another human's company, we try and make it impossible for the other person to escape the relationship. I hate this weak species. **MIND**
****

You know how it is, man. You wake up in the morning and you just want to scream yourself back to sleep. You attempt to come up with a reason not to go to work or school, so that you don't have to be around any other humans. Eventually, you have to drag yourself out of the house; since you couldn't come up with a single valid reason to stay home. The day out there in the hellhole sucks you dry of energy and you get real shitty with anyone you come into contact with. That feeling of self hatred, you fool, the need to self mutilate, it's just what they want you to feel. Never give in.

…

I know that if I try hard enough, I can keep going. I have the strength to keep going, but that doesn't help motivate me to trudge passively. Sometimes I enjoy the pain. I punched myself in the jaw last night, and I keep pushing on the swollen bruise to make it hurt more. Someone in class asked what I was doing, I told them I was pleasuring myself. Anything is a good distraction from the migraines – the bad pain. I know the migraines are only a product of my weakness; and I know they will go away once I am stronger. I cannot allow myself to be weak like all of you because then I will get crushed under the shoe of some higher-up. I turn to the iron and the books, while you turn to the bottle and the needle.

****

I'm really tired and it's late at night, but my mind is too loud to try and sleep. I can't stop thinking and I think that I might keep thinking and thinking until my brain shrivels-up and dies. I want to sleep without waking for a couple of years. I want to take a vacation in the world that I see when I close my eyes. My world is a strange reality made of distorted memories and abstract thought – and I love it. I would love to float around my own mind for the rest of eternity if I could. In my mind, I can make anything happen. A planet of aliens who breathe sulfur instead of oxygen, or a world full of misery, pain, depression, and rage. Split open skulls littering the ground, collapsed lungs and disease. Gray skies, oceans of oil that burn eternally, and napalm destroyed forests. I don't care how dark it is, as long as it's mine. As long as it's far away from the hellhole. The people in my mind are more real than any of the mutants I encounter at school daily. Zombie freaks walk the halls and try to eat my flesh. I need to repel those braindead fools. I'm only building these walls to accomplish the task of isolation from the enemy. Don't mind the sign posted out front that says, "HELP". It was supposed to say "FUCK OFF", but the artist who drew it up only speaks Italian and my original message got lost in translation. They should not be graced by my presence, since they cannot possibly live up to my hypocritical standards.

****

2:04 AM:　　　Tonight's late night soundtrack is one of my favorite albums from Steely Dan. The album is *The Royal Scam*, and it's infinitely better than anything the Deftones or Green Day have ever put out. The specific track playing at this moment is one of my many theme songs: "The Caves of Altamira". Tonight as I write I feel like an only man in a desert tundra. There is nothing but frozen sand for miles and everything is pitch black, and yet your image is still ever so clear to me now. I can vividly see your sharp talons digging into my forearm. The pain is nothing. I can smell the stench of your acid venom burning my flesh. We have never met in person, but I know that you await me. My Naima turned Calahoochi by the moon's scowl.

. . .

Her name was Phala. She was completely alienated at school and came to hate her peers because of that fact. Phala cut herself every night and told people it was her cat whenever asked (which was rare). One day, I got to meet Phala. I told her that she should try killing herself. I always do that to the people I like the most. Then one day, later that month, Phala got on top of the school. I was conveniently passing by on my bike when she jumped off. Her blood, guts, and bone shards spattered the nine foot radius where her body had hit the concrete. I stopped at the impact, and scooped up some of her blood into an empty plastic sandwich bag I had in my pocket. That was five years ago, and I still have her blood in this little baggie. It's all brown and dried-up now, but I still love it.

****

I told the guys in biology about how romantic relationships in high school are just shallow power trips. It came up when MJ spoke about his lack of a girlfriend. Chris asked me who hurt me for me to say what I had said. I did not have an answer for him then, but I do now. I believe I hurt myself. I use my own pessimism and solipsism to tear myself apart. Whenever a girl talks to me in the halls, I get the hell out of there as quickly as possible and repeat my famous mantra inside my head, "No! Bad Adal!". All I can see is expensive dates, torture, and misery in the eyes of high school girls. I know how that shit would end already. It kind of reminds me of "Fool" by Rollins Band. I know that I can't relate to any of those people. Ignorance is bliss, but I would much rather have all this knowledge and feel like… Adal. I know things that cut me open and pour salt in the wound.

…

There's this person in one of my classes who hates me for some reason. Whatever, can't have everyone kissing your ass. Her disdain for me seems to grow everytime I open my mouth. She probably hates me because I'm a pessimistic asshole who brings everyone around me down. I would rather be me than her though.

****

My tribal mask, I wear it always when exploring the alien planet. I wear the mask as a symbol of my people and my culture. My people are the people of the sun. We acknowledge the sun as the one and only true God in this solar system. The alien people around here don't like my religion. They keep trying to shove white Jesus and American football up my ass, and down my throat. They are all the people of the screen. My tribal mask is a middle finger to them. I walk around their world with that middle finger proudly displayed. I don't really give a fuck what you think about it.

****

It was another cold day in hell. I was full of rage and hatred; as well as a burning ire for everything around me. I sat atop my stoop, looking down at the world below me, waiting for it to burn. A heroine whom I have never once respected came along and sat beside me. I was very deep into my brooding and wished only to be left alone. "Get away from me, you damnable whore." I said. Despite my cold tone, she did not move. Instead she turned toward me, punched me in the jaw, and

proceeded to tell me something that I will never forget. "I haven't come here for your abuse or amusement – I have come here to tell you what you really are. You are just a pessimistic and hateful person who tries to take others down to your pitiful level, just so you can feel a little less alone. You just sit there on your damn stoop, hating everything, and acting like you're better than everyone. I know, however, that you are no better than the worst parts of society. People like you are truly the scum of the Earth. You are like a damn parasite; feeding off the happiness of everyone around you. I feel completely disgusted by your presence alone. The mere sight of you makes me sick to my stomach. I wish you a long and agonizing death; for you do not even deserve a quick and painless end!" She finally prances off with that fucking self-satisfied walk of hers. A man coming from the direction the heroine had just went in passed by moments later and stopped to ask me what had just happened. "Excuse me sir, I just happened to notice that beautiful woman walking away from here in a huff. Did something bad happen over here?" I responded to the man's question without looking up into his eyes, because mine were full of tears, and I didn't want him to see. "Wasn't nothin' man, just a small debate."
****

If you could see yourself the way I see you, then you would probably commit suicide. You're such a microscopic, brainless, useless peon. Your entire value as a person doesn't even equivalent to a single American penny. By the time I'm done with you here, you will wish that you were never born. You'll disintegrate into the Egyptian sands. I will not kill you, but you will be dead on the inside by the time this is over with. I will tell you things that will make you vomit blood and bile. My words will strike like multiple baseball bats and crowbars. Your flesh will become mine. My hand will cut you with the very knife that you gave me. I will be feasting upon your flesh tonight. I am once again telling you, you will not die by my physical hand. But you will die. You won't want to live anymore; too scared to face the reality of it all. I want you to hate not only yourself, but hate me as well – and at the same time – you will want me even more than you hate me or yourself. And when you are finally dead, oh God, the things I'll do to that corpse.

****

"It's the thing that only eats hippies!" If such a thing really existed, it would be my favorite animal. No more "alternative" coffee shops, no more PETAphiles.

****

I participated in some rather interesting activities before school. The nature of these activities is unimportant to the story; though it is related. I remember walking into class, but not how I got there. I took a seat at my desk. A girl wearing black wire frame glasses walked into the room. I thought it was someone I knew, and almost complimented her on the new spectacles, but I soon realized it wasn't who I thought it was. Then I noticed a girl standing at a desk parallel to mine. She was wearing nothing but a plain, white bra. The girl started stabbing herself in the chest with a hand-crank drill. There was no blood however, just gaping black holes wherever she stabbed. I started to feel dizzy and then, all of a sudden, I was standing five inches in front of her. We were now in an almost completely empty room with only a bright incandescent shop light hanging above our heads and the wooden desk she had been standing at. The room was shrouded in darkness and appeared to go on forever. I touched her. She continued to stand there in suspended animation, as I moved in close I put my left arm around her torso; with my right hand darting between her legs. She was now completely naked and I started to lick her neck. She tasted and felt oh so real. Her face stayed completely blank and emotionless, as we rubbed closely together. Then, out of nowhere, I was compelled to drop to the concrete floor. I got on my stomach and started to rub my body against the freezing cold ground. One of my weights appeared before my face and I started to lick it, while still rubbing against the floor. Finally and abruptly, I wake up. The first thing I do is check the time; it is 8:40 AM. Only 45 minutes before I have to be at school. What a motherfucking dream.

****

Call me Scum of the Earth sweetheart.

Yep, I'm the one who raped that woman behind the club. Yes sir, I'm the motherfucker who molested that girl on the steps of her highschool. I'm the crooked sonofabitch who pays the women working for my company barely more than half of what I pay my guys. I started the war and slaughtered all those people for no good reason. Yeah girl, I'm the Scum of the Earth.

****

Fuck December. This month and the four to succeed it can all go choke on it. They're the coldest and most useless months here in the midwest. I don't know why anyone would grow-up here, and then on their own, decide to continue living here for the rest of their lives. This is where people meet unremarkable ends. This is where people slowly rot at their nine to five jobs. Fuck this whole part of the country.

…

It was a beautiful summer evening. I rode a skateboard past the school. Despite having no experience riding a skateboard ever, I was riding with amazing grace and excellent, consistent velocity. School had just let out and students crowded the sidewalk I was riding on. They all looked so real. I narrowly avoided colliding with a group of them, causing me to fall off the skateboard. I got up, uninjured, and continued riding. The dream gets kind of strange, with some details I'd rather not remember, and then I wake up at 8:32 AM. I almost started bawling when I came to the full realization that what had just happened had only been a dream. Even pleasant dreams turn into nightmares in the winter. They only remind me of how much I miss the summertime.

****

I told her that she looks even more magnificent without all that crappy makeup. She returned my compliment by ripping out my tongue and eating it whole. She pushed me down the west stairwell and shot me in the back once I reached the bottom. She came down the stairs, stood me up against the wall, pulled my pants down, and proceeded to bite my testicles off. She used my own freshly sharpened pencil to stab my eyes out. She chopped off my feet and hit me in the solar plexus with a steel baseball bat. She kissed me. She tied me up and took me to the old Darden Bridge. She warmly embraced my battered body and wept softly over my shoulder. Finally, she jumped off of the bridge, down into the deep dark abyss; with me still in her arms.

…

I'm going to explode. I feel like a single grain of sand in an otherwise squeaky clean sink. My eyes sting from a lack of sleep. I had another dream last night. I cannot remember what it was about, but I woke up wanting to go back into the world of the dream. I am convinced that it was a nightmare. "John Wayne was a nazi", what a thing to say. I don't know if the gun-toting hillbilly was a nazi or not, so I guess I'll just take MDC's word for it.

****

I'm becoming a Nihilist. Reality is completely pointless. There is no destiny or fate. You either fuck, marry, and die; or you tear shit up and then die. Time is like a glass window. The present is like a medium-sized stone hitting that window. The resulting cracks are possibilities for the future. There are so many cracks because nothing lest death is certain, and there is always a choice. If I were to kill one of these walking, talking insects out there, the chances are pretty high that I would be sent to prison after a "speedy" trial. But, perhaps I get away with it. That's a somewhat unprecedented outcome of first-degree murder, but it's possible. I know that was an extreme example, but death is never far from my mind, so that's what I write. The farther out the cracks are, the smaller and harder they are to see. It's best not to focus too much on the cracks, however, and just pay close attention to the stone; and who's throwing it.

****

It isn't fair, and that's a fact. That's what I was always told and have learnt from experience anyway. And yet whenever someone sees me reading in the stairwell, they cry "Unfair!". Then it becomes the "everyone must be equals" game. But you see, I don't play that shit. The asshole who sells dope out of the bathroom and me are not equals. The weak piece of shit who buys that dope and uses it to make all of his problems go away is nowhere near my level. Fuck being equals, we can do that shit when you all learn some goddamn common sense.

INTERMISSION 3:

THE RAMBLING POEM I

Sometimes
I think that I am full of it
I convince myself that I'm filth
I believe everything I tell myself
That means it must be true
Right?
Whatever
Have you ever looked yourself in the eyes
Like, with a mirror
Did it make you feel like
"Who the hell is this guy?
Why does he look like that?
I ought to punch his lights out."
Don't answer
I know you have
Oh
I almost forgot about you
I started talking to myself there
Why do you read this shit anyway?
Did you recognize my name on the cover?
Maybe
You know this particular piece was written in the summer?
Yep
As of writing, it is July 25, 2022
It's currently 2:04 AM, eastern daylight time
I thought about killing myself
A few times before
Glad I didn't do it
Then I wouldn't be able to…
To make you laugh like this
This is
Afterall
My own Divine Comedy

Just,
You know
Without the hell and heaven shtick
Only purgatory
And comedy
Look at you
Reading like some little bitch
How old are you anyway?
15? 20? 35?
Am I even in range?
Actually
I don't really give fuck
"Age is just a number"
That's what R Kelly said
And what the priest said
When I was three years old
Remember?
Oh right
You weren't there
Well
Um
Laugh
You know you love my jokes
I'm hilarious
The first poetic act break was Super Jesus
This one is late night ramblings
Hope you like it

TRUE TALES OF ADOLESCENCE PT. 2

I was once again at Jerome's uncle's house. A few months had passed since the prostitute debacle, and it was now mid-autumn. Jerome, his uncle, and I were all just sitting on the couch; talking shit and having fun. Although I was still somewhat terrified of Jerome's uncle, I had grown accustomed to hanging around him and the rest of the big boys from the north side of town.

I had to be home by 7:30 PM, so when time drifted itself to about 6:50 PM, I decided I better head home. For some reason, Jerome's uncle would always bum out a little whenever it was time for me to leave. This time was no different, and he did not want to let me leave. Maybe he liked me because of how different I was from the rest of them, me being a square and all; who knows?

So anyway, I hopped on my expensive, chrome, BMX bike and started toward home. The temperature outside was maybe 45 degrees fahrenheit, and being infected by my father's reptile blood made it feel more like 20 – so I was anxious and ready to get home. As I zipped down Cleveland toward home, I noticed a blue minivan trying to make a left turn off Hastings, which is perpendicular to Cleveland. I thought that they wouldn't be turning off for at least a whole minute after I had already crossed their path, since traffic on Cleveland was somewhat tightly packed.

What I had not factored in was the impatience and possible irritation of the driver in the blue minivan. The car took-off just as I crossed in front of them. I remember my complete and utter shock as I was flung from my bike, right onto the street. I laid on the street for a few seconds, just pondering what had just happened to me, and how easily it could have been avoided, until the middle-age woman driving the blue mini van ran out of her car to help walk me to the sidewalk.

When we reached the sidewalk, the woman began apologizing profusely. Being the innocent little kid I was, I told her that it was okay; since I had at the time thought the accident was all my fault. The lady calls 911 and I decide to call my dad on the hand-me-down phone my mother had very recently given me. I only got as far as telling my dad that I had been hit on Cleveland before he had hung-up. My house was probably a one or two-minute drive from the spot I had been hit; my dad got there in his black, 1996 Impala SS in no more than 30 seconds.

My father was sure to inspect that I wasn't mortally wounded (which I wasn't) before going over my bike. The brakes were locked up. This, of course, is a simple fix, but it only made my father even more angry. If it had been a male driver who had hit me and not that woman, things might have gotten ugly.

The baconators arrived and when speaking to my dad, said the woman wasn't at fault because of a "tree blocking her view". (I have since driven down that street in my own car and can testify that the tree they spoke of does not obscure the driver's view of the sidewalk.) They also said that the accident was really my fault.

Yes, this was the fault of the ten-year-old kid, not the thirty something year old adult. They said I was supposed to stop before crossing, even though this was not an intersection, and I had no stop sign; while the lady in the blue minivan had one indeed. I got in my father's car and watched him argue for about fifteen minutes before he gave up, put my bike in the trunk of the Impala, and left the scene. And they wonder why I ride with such fury and velocity now.

CHAPTER 4:
Black Winter

As they walk past
I catch a whiff
A strange,
Pungent odor
A mixture of perfume and…
Vomit
So skinny
So boney
Like a chicken that's all skin
They stop to conversate
The smell of vomit grows stronger
Try the perfume shield all you want
But I know
What happened to last night's dinner
And this morning's breakfast
I'm not shaming you
You've already done that yourself
Fuck social media
Fuck a magazine
Fuck a corporate fatcat
****

Whilst traversing the desolate halls of my hell, I came upon four snickering mutant demons. They called me a weirdo as I walked past them. This put a grin on my face. If I'm weird from the enemy's perspective, then my mission is going great. Throughout my very few years of being on this mudball, I have picked up on the fact that not doing the popular thing in life is considered weird. The popular activities of my generation include, but are not limited to, doing copious amounts of drugs, putting in the least amount of effort into anything and everything, playing on a smartphone, and acting a complete damn fool. So if they recognise me as not being down with any of those *wonderful* things, then I am doing fucking fantastic.
****

This is my Black Winter
All I can see is black

The temperature is hate
There is no escape from the darkness
Nothing to warm up from hate
No bike to ride
No road to ride on anyway
White is black
Black is invisible
A prelude to death
****

Watching my fellow ape-brained males doing pull-ups on the bar the recruiters set up in the cafeteria has become a new self-indulgent pleasure of mine. They were all taking turns, trying to do as many pull-ups as possible in order to impress the girls and each other. Chase and I just sat back laughing – thinking about how many of them we could destroy with a single airstrike. The mutants act like they're tough shit. They always make sure to demonstrate their fake gangster attitude. I wish I was allowed to bash their puny little brains in. I think it would be hilarious if two cars – one full of bloods, the other full of crips – came and shot up the place as the fake little gangsters are all scrambling into their buses. They bring their little knives and guns to school; as if that will protect them when death comes running. I wish they could see themselves the way I see them; maybe then the ignorance would stop.
****

"Hey Britany!" Drew said excitedly. "Your hair looks really nice today." Brittany immediately started to bleed out of her eyes, mouth, nose, and ears. Blood kept pouring out until all of it was drained from her body, and then all her organs and bones came out of her mouth. Drew said to himself, "Oh well, guess I'll go find someone else to talk to." and walked away. He wandered through the halls until he was tired of wandering, at which time the bell denoting the beginning of third period rang. Drew entered his third period class and sat down in a seat across from his pal, MJ. "Hey MJ", Drew stated glumly, "How's your day been so far?" MJ, instead of responding, started to swell-up like a balloon. After twenty seconds, MJ exploded like an overinflated bike innertube. Blood, guts, and shards of bone went flying everywhere. Some of the

bone shards went right through Drew's classmates like stray bullets, so Drew decided to split the scene. Throughout the rest of the day, Drew kept on trying to conversate with person after person – all of whom met terribly tragic fates. One girl turned inside-out, another person's stomach exploded, and one guy even fell apart like a Potato Head. Eventually, Drew went into the school bathroom, looked into the mirror, and said, "Hey Drew, go fuck yourself." Shortly after, Drew's head exploded. Later on, some students found him on the bathroom floor, in front of the sink, with a gun in his right hand and his cranium blown clean off. "Boy Chris, Drew really was an outcast; wasn't he?" "Whatever MJ. Let's just go smoke our shit in a different bathroom."
****

The Jungle
Dark and rainy
Humid and foggy
I keep my hand
On the hilt of my saber
Scary creatures hide in the foliage
Mutants
Animals
Call them what you will
They'll all get cut-down
****

He broke up with me. We were sitting atop the steps of our school, as usual, just tripping passerby and laughing about it. But after our third or fourth victim, he grabbed me and threw me down the stairs. I could only lay there, with my ribs poking through my lungs, my skull cracked wide open, and watch as he went into hysterics. Before walking away, he said to me, "It's over. Fuck you bitch."
****

I'm wandering around this rainforest; wasted off the Black Winter blues. I have the Snort my Load LP by Nig Heist playing through the earbuds right now. Most would call Nig Heist grotesque, but all their jokes are just satirical views on life.

Today I was standing outside a doorway that leads into a short dead-end hallway, with the ceramics room, my destination, at the end. I was just waiting for the traffic jam to clear out, when this dumbass-looking girl stopped in front of me. She stares at me with this braindead expression; mouth agape, eyes wide open. I glared into her glassy zombie eyes, hoping to get her to go away. She eventually left, after about fifteen full seconds of staring at me. They are all so used to just texting each other; they don't even know how to talk to someone in real life.
****

I laid there in the middle of the sidewalk, blood pouring from my right side. All the people walking past just pointed and laughed at my misery. That was only three minutes ago, but it feels as if it's been three hours. I'm still laying here, on the sidewalk, and passersby are still laughing at me. The thought that I am going to die has only just now occurred to me a few seconds ago. Funny how we don't think of death until we're on his doorstep. But I want to live, so I'm holding my breath. Maybe if I never take my last breath, then I will never die.
****

My sight is an alien view of reality
I don't see what they see
They see a beautiful rainbow
I see glorious storm clouds
They appear as mutants to me
Zombified by ChatSnap and Tic Tac
They don't like my book and I,
I really don't give a flying fuck
I walk alone through the abyss
Sometimes I feel chained to that abyss
I'm chained to nothingness
Serving a lifetime in their world
****

I'm such a hypocrite. I think about you when I lift weights. I've talked so much shit and yet, you stay on my mind. The cold makes me think about you. I think about your shallow existence and it makes me hate myself. What I feel for you is something between hatred and resentment. My contempt for you is staggering. I do not know how to deal with any of this, so I stand here behind the safety of this glass door, staring at the snow and thinking of what I would say to you if you were here with me.

"You don't have to get naked for me. I watch you shower every night." That is what God said to me the night I came home with Him from the bar.
****

On my planet, I am normal. Everyone is into late night literature soundtracks and long bike rides to nowhere. We do not wage wars. We do not have nations, nor leaders. There is no currency because we all love what we do and do it for ourselves. The men are men, the women are women – no weaklings like you have here on Earth. My people do not hate one another, but we do not bother trying to love one another either. Someday my people will come here and live on Earth. The hydrogen and helium in our atmosphere is starting to become quite bothersome and Earth seems to have just the right conditions for us to thrive – more or less. I just have to finish making this pesticide first.
****

He kept trying to tell her that what he was saying was the truth. Joe tried telling her for the hundredth time that he wasn't just with her for the sex. "I tell you that I just want someone to love, and though you can hear my words clearly, you do not listen to what I am trying to say. Anytime I tell you that I just want us to hang out over at my place, the only thing you can think of is an invitation for sexual intercourse. I suppose I can understand why you are this way though. After years of misogynistic tyranny, you've been led to the conclusion that all any guy wants to do is fuck; but I promise that it isn't true. I will never make you perform for me. We can just be there for each other. I will not lie to you, I have never loved before and I don't know what two people are supposed to do when they're in love, but we can find out together." She tells Joe that she's heard it all before. A tear falls from Joe's right eye as he continues his lamenting plea. "No no, this isn't just some trick! Not every guy is in it to smash and dash, and I would never ask you to do something that you're uncomfortable with. Those other guys are weak –

they drag us real, genuine men down. The worst of a group typically speaks the loudest and crooked people know how to sneak their way far up the ladder. I'm not like that, most of us aren't. I'm afraid you've got the wrong man." Joe kisses her on the cheek one final time, and leaves her house – with a waterfall of tears flowing down his face.
****

I was sitting in the stairwell once again, peacefully enjoying *Pimp: The Story of My Life* by Iceberg Slim. A group of three – or maybe it was four – girls walks in. One of them tries talking to me, but I ignore her and continue reading my book. They sit across from me, on the other side of the divider rail, and start talking amongst themselves. Their babbling forces my mind to connect them to the women in *Pimp*. About a minute after their arrival in the stairwell, a security guard named Bill comes to take them back to class. Bill the security guard tells the girls to go back from whence they came, they do not budge. Bill walks away, and they giggle maniacally and continue talking. The realization that these freaks of nature weren't going anywhere, anytime soon, occurs to me – so I decide to leave the once so quiet and peaceful stairwell. I quietly close my book, gather my folders and notebooks from the step below me, and begin to head out. As I get up from my comfortable stoop, one of the girls apologizes to me. I tell her that it's okay, even though I wanted to tell her to fuck off. She asks me my name, I tell her, and she says it's a nice name. I finally tell her thanks and get the hell out of there.
****

I was in fifth grade. My fists yearned to slam into his face. He tried to run, but I took off my jacket, used it as a whip, and tripped him with it. I grabbed the scrawny, four foot nine, kid and started jabbing him in the ribs. I can't remember everything I did in that moment – I've spent a good part of my youth trying to forget – but I do remember slamming him into a closed locker and beating on his back like it were a tribal drum. After a few minutes of relentless beating, I threw him to the tiled floor. All he could do was lay there, crying, as I watched in sick satisfaction; happy from the petty revenge I had just gotten. A teacher walked out into the hallway, and I can still see her look of total shock and horror as she retreated back into her classroom. I will never know what that scene looked like from her perspective. I got a stern talking to from the vice principal the next day, and that was it. No suspension, no detention.

****

I was walking down the empty salted sidewalk one freezing January evening, when she appeared out of nowhere. I later came to find out her name was Margarette. I tried to step around her, but she would not let me pass. Out of irritation I yelled, "Dammit woman! What's your problem?" Margarette told me that she had been waiting out there for quite a while, just to see me. I pulled out my gun, and shot her point-blank in the forehead. What, you thought this was some love story or some shit? No man, this right here is real fucking life I'm talking about. No love, only lust, greed, and murder.

****

He was a loner. The people he had to deal with in life aggravated him greatly. He went to school Monday through Friday, just like everyone else, and got his ass kicked Sunday through Saturday. He never fought back because he was too scared, and he also never wanted to hurt anyone. He didn't hate himself the way the rest of America hated themselves. He exercised, ate healthy, and kept his mind sharp from the books he loved to read. He didn't talk to girls all too often – they all made him feel like lowly scum. He always wished that he weren't attracted to them. One day, he came home with a cracked rib. He finished off the last two pages of the book he had been reading at the time, and shot himself in the head with his mother's handgun.

She was a social butterfly. She was less vain than the average teenager. She didn't wear thick layers of crappy makeup, or follow the latest fashion trends. She did whatever she damn well pleased and said fuck all to internet fads. She had many friends – all of whom were far less intelligent than her – and she enjoyed their company. She never bothered anyone who didn't want to be bothered. One day, someone she cared for deeply died; and she fell apart completely. The man who had died was like another father to her. She now saw reality in a far more dim light. She didn't go to school for a week. When she did eventually return, her depression was so thick that dark clouds appeared to revolve

around her head. One day, she decided to slit her throat in her room. It took an excruciatingly long sixty seconds for her to die.
****

"You're taller than your sister." She wondered what had possessed that motherfucker to make such a blunt remark. She followed him home that night and burnt his house down while he slept. What would you do?
****

Poetry blues featuring Coltrane
Tired and broken down
Gone and dead
The years stand still
You pass through them
A wandering soul
A fall leaf in the breeze
No direction
It's one of those nights
The monkey is on your back
You're all worn-out
You find me
We embrace
I kiss you
You slip out of my arms
The breeze has swept you back up
Floating endlessly in the cold air
****

None of them are worth our time. Aliens like us have no use for any of them. They are just poisonous, zombie mutants. We don't ever need to talk to them again, because we can just talk to each other. We can watch them. We can just sit here until the end of time; joking and laughing as the humans slowly die-off and fade away.

...

I open my mouth to talk, but I have no vocal chords to speak with. Perhaps it is time for me to stop coming here, for I have nothing left to give away. I'm all bones now that I have given away my flesh, my

organs, blood, and soul. My skeleton is the most intriguing thing to have ever graced this spot with its presence. Occasionally, someone will take a bone or two as souvenirs. "Hey mommy, look what I got!" says Billy, "It's a real alien bone!" "Yeah, whatever." says mommy, as she takes another gulp of that 40oz of beer.
****

Blood starts flowing down her leg as she rinses her hair in the shower. "What the hell?" she says to herself out loud, "I just had my period last week!" Then a huge serpent starts to emerge from between her thighs. The woman screams out in terror and pain as she falls to the floor. The massive, 16 feet long python slowly slithers all the way out of the woman. Once fully emerged, it devours the woman whole and says in a deep, regal voice, "Now, how do you like it?"
****

Falling fast
Falling quiet
Screaming silently
All the way down
Things try and grab me
To stop me from falling
But I maneuver away from them
I shift in midair
I'm headed for the abyss
The abyss which is so beautiful
A gorgeous void of black
****

Just me and my Literature Blues
They fill up my head
They weigh down my shoes
Time spent thinking about them
Is time I lose
I hate laying in my bed
I wish to explore the world
But when I look at the world
All I see is red

I don't prefer your views
I just want to do this my way
They tell me my way is wrong
Well,
I think that their way is wrong
****

    She pushed me off of the bridge – right into the rushing water below. Just minutes before, we had been talking about murdering mindless mutant morons and slaughtering stupid sonaofabitches. She tried to kiss me, but I jolted away from her voluptuous lips. Tears welled-up in her eyes, and she started yelling at me; about how I think she's ugly. I tried to explain myself, in a vain attempt to calm her down. I told her that she's the most beautiful girl I've ever seen, and that I'm only scared of hurting her, but she didn't seem to understand. That is when, in her blind rage, she finally pushed me off the bridge. All of that happened a few months ago. I'm still here at the bottom of the river; and I'm never coming back to the surface.

    Down here, I see things through dead concrete eyes. I have become one of the bricks under the river. All I do nowadays is stare up into the void which I used to call home. I see right past the murky waters and fish passing by, right into the empty space that is the surface world. The void has become a disease. It's consuming my flesh down to bone. I feel that one day, I will be reduced to nothingness. I don't want to talk to any of those people, up there on the surface. All I can do is watch as they pass on the bridge overhead. Sometimes I try to look away, but my concrete eyes will not move.
****

    She was naked – that is to say that she had no skin. Her name was Charlene. She had no clothes on either, just bare muscle tissue. There was a copious amount of blood dripping off her bodacious body. I too had no flesh nor clothes. We slept together – though very little sleeping actually took place. We took bites out of each other all night. Her blood was rich in iron – such a divine taste. The next day she left town for some job opportunity. It was a crazy realistic dream.
****

It was a Black Winter. Veronica found herself talking to a female human. The human said that she had been raped by her father when she was only three years old. The human said that even though it had happened so long ago, when she was only a toddler at that, she could still vividly see her bastard father's disgusting cock on all other men; as if everything had just happened yesterday. No matter how hard she tried, she could not delete the image from her mind. She said that she would never have children. For whatever reason, the human tried to kiss Veronica. As a habitual reflex, Veronica kneed the human in the chest. The human hanged herself later that night. They say that high temperatures are to blame for so much of the insanity in the world, but I say that the cold is the true culprit.

INTERMISSION 4:

SUPER JESUS II

I am the sinner eviscerator
I am the ultimate judge
And the executioner
I am none other than,
Super Jesus!
With the power of divine sight
And my superior might
I shall seek out
And crush all in doubt
Non-believers better beware
Whenever I exit my heavenly lair
No!
That is no plane
Nor a flying train
Not a missile
Or a flaming asteroid
It is the Mega Christ!
Come to bathe the world
In undeserved divinity
You shall suffer for your sins
The priests have told you nothing but lies
There is no such thing as forgiveness

VENUS'S DEPRESSION

Venus sits just out of reach
High in the sky
Out in the universe
Surrounded by nothingness
She is a fiery planet
Hottest in the solar system
Thick walls to keep everyone out
Thick walls to keep everything in
Loneliest planet of all
No life within her atmosphere
No explorers anxious to set foot on her surface
Not even a moon to keep her company
She pretends to like it this way
But deep down inside
She doesn't want things to be like this
Some can see her alienation in the sky
Others can relate
But no one comes to help
Venus is all alone
On her own

CHAPTER 5:
Set it on Fire!

The child had been anointed in the literature. She wandered through the void, and through the abyss, looking for someone who wasn't there. She was alone in every space she occupied. Other humans had never interested her, not in the least bit. She only spoke to the west facing brick wall of her run-down, studio apartment. She would say things like, "You are my only friend" and "I love you Brick". Brick was the name she had given the wall. Her philosophy was that anything being spoken to ought to have a name. She didn't love or hate either of her parents. Her mother died when the child was fifteen years old and she never shed a single tear. Her father got really fucked-up on cough syrup that same week and tried to molest her. She broke four of his ribs and he never tried anything that stupid again. Today, she's in her early 30s. She still lives in the same cruddy apartment that she's been living in since she was twenty. She has never tried looking for someone to be with, nor will she ever. She hates the feeling of her own skin and only touches herself to get clean. She works downtown, at a convenience store. Her favorite and most frequent passtime nowadays is playing with a gun that she found one night, at the mouth of a dark alleyway. It's a revolving pistol. The pistol has had two remaining bullets left in the chamber since she found it. She spends sleepless nights sucking on the barrel of the pistol, with her index finger rubbing the trigger. She does this for hours at a time most nights. The woman who I am referring to lives on the other side of the world. You won't find her here.

****

Sometimes your own world wraps you up so tight that you forget about the real world around you. The pessimism takes full effect and you can't escape your own mind. You turn to nothingness. You melt into the pages of your book and become the words. All you can see is the paper. The abyss consumes you and you're just glad that something finally holds onto you, without making you feel like less than a person.

...

I sit here atop my stoop, isolated and at peace. All I ever feel when I'm around those people is alienation. It's not their fault though. They're just all so strange to me because of everything they say and do. I'm perfectly content just sitting here and creating a new world for

myself. The best things happen when you're alone. Books, music, long bike rides – they are all best enjoyed alone. I am alone. Alone defines me. I am a lone brick and I have concrete eyes.
****

Negativity
Why do humans hate it so?
They say to be positive
They tell me my negativity is bad
But in reality
Negativity is just a plain view of the world
Being positive too often is a waste of time
Optimism is weakness
Manifestation?
Fuck you
If you're going to do something
Then do it
But don't go on with some damn mantra
Or some weak-ass prayers
It makes you look ridiculous
****

Coltrane and book, complete with isolation and divine light. I'm floating on a slow breeze, drifting to nowhere. Inside myself I find nothing but pent-up opportunity. I'm ready to hurry-up and finish writing this book, and then publish it. Fuck the slow breeze shit, actually, I'm going to go fast. I want the life, my life, any life but yours. Through my eyes, aimless college, dead-end jobs, mortgages and families are the enemy. I'm currently listening to Alabama by John Coltrane – perfect for igniting my determination. That middle class shit isn't for me, honey. I want to explore the world, and I can't do that on some pitiful twenty dollars an hour paycheck.
****

We had a mutual hatred for each other. We tried to kill each other constantly. They tried to separate us at school, it didn't work. We did some stuff together once. During which, I attempted to stab her in the back of the neck, while she tried to gouge my eyes out. I was initially

confused when she killed herself a couple of weeks ago. I have since realized that she did so, only so that I may never have the satisfaction of killing her myself.
******

I was in class. Someone had stolen something from off my desk and I wanted to know who that someone was. I got up out of my seat, and told Chase that I was going to pull out the perpetrator's tongue, strangle them with it, and use their battered corpse as a punching bag. Then, as I sat back down, two people proceeded to steal things right off of my desk – right before my very eyes. One of them was a guy, the other a girl. They had taken something each and ran toward the doorway of the classroom. I chase them to the doorway and once there, I am met with a horde of students entering the classroom – causing me to lose track of the thieves. Just then, I spot a girl who I've gone to school with since elementary. For some reason, I feel the carnal inclination to attack the girl and before I know it, she's laying down on the floor with me on top of her. I knew that the girl had done nothing to me and yet, I hurt her all the same. The girl says my name repeatedly and blocks all of my punches as I try to maul her – like some sort of animal. People in the background are politely asking me to stop. I start biting the girl's neck and shoulders, and then I turn into a giant green monster. Now, I'm holding the girl in one arm and using the other to climb a nearby bookcase. Someone from within the gathered crowd of students and teachers below yells, "Bad!", in the same way you would while correcting a dog. I climb down the bookcase, and sit the girl down on the ground. I begin to tear-up and repeat, "Bad?", like a toddler.
******

Traversing the endless green void
The abyss, filled with fake foliage
Strange creatures lurk around every corner
One slowly creeps toward me
It is an animal of great beauty
It is a gorgeous bird
With feathers colored a brilliantly, incandescent gold
I extend my hand out toward the phoenix

I yearn to touch its wing
The majestic creature bites off my finger
Then it flies off, back into the void
Never to be seen again
I continue my trudge into the green void
Blood now gushing from my right hand
The smell attracts shark-like organisms
They gather and walk beside me
They pretend to be herbivores
They're just wolves in sheep's clothing
They shed their costumes and attack
They maul my body down to bone
They slink away
Pleased with what they have done
Now, with nothing more to lose
Nothing more to give-away
I sit down on a fake tree stump
Now and forever rotting away, all alone
****

Damn you all to hell
All of your little voices, screaming
Moronic chants from your favorite "artists"
And all the while your messiahs all worship yet another god
God in the form of cold, hard cash
Every one of you is blind
****

It bums me out everytime I get to thinking about girls. I know this is a foolish thought because of my youth, but the feeling of suicidal pessimism that they leave me with seems so real. I don't see what most guys see in pretty girls. Whenever I see one, I stare right past the outer beauty – I see right down to the hidden pain infliction and misery consumption. I've never been one for misogyny. I do not hate women, rather, I hate myself around them. It is also my growing suspicion that no one ever loves anyone, aside from maybe their own family. Humans have the irrational fear of dying alone, so we go to tremendous lengths to ensure that we drag someone to the grave with us. Everything that a man might do to keep his girlfriend is not done to her benefit, but done so that the man is not left alone. We inflict pain upon ourselves and the ones we're with by cramming lies down our own throats and theirs; just so that we can attempt to hold on to a slippery relationship. We consume our own misery when we are inevitably left by whoever we were once with. It is these thoughts that have made all dreams of relationships with anyone nightmares for me.

****

She was sixteen. She sat alone everywhere she went. She hated everyone outside of her own mind. She only loved herself, nature, and the sun. No plant or animal ever told her a lie; never stole from her or messed with her personally. The sun always shows its true colors, and it never pushes clouds out of the way when they obscure it from view. The girl liked these qualities. And she, like her idols, always told it how it was. If she thought you were a fat, loud-mouthed piece of shit pig, then she would tell you so. She despised her parents. Her mother was a crotchety old bitch of a high school teacher, who terrorized the students she taught. Her dad was a weak, piece of shit drug addict and alcoholic who was constantly out of work. She took long bike rides alone. She liked riding mile after mile without stopping. She especially enjoyed riding along the river. She once saw a boy about her age crouched-down at the foot of the river, talking to a turtle. He was telling the turtle how much he envied the turtle's existence, since the turtle wasn't even aware that it did indeed exist. Their eyes met briefly and they both grinned. Maybe she started talking to him, or he started talking to her, the specific details don't matter much. The important thing is that one convinced the other that they should both die together. They met in her room that night and simultaneously, they shot one another in the forehead.

****

I don't want to be the first man to set foot on Mars, rather, I want to be the first to die there. Wouldn't that be something? To die completely alone, the only life form for millions of miles around. To be the first human not to die on Earth, but also not in some spaceship. To

die in a completely new frontier. My death would be the one thing that will never belong to them – it would belong to the stars.
****

       They are all so especially ignorant sometimes. They make me lose all hope for my generation. "Women who watch female prison shows are closeted lesbians!" She kept on fucking saying that, very loudly, to her friend. The freak just repeated it over and over like a damn broken vinyl record. Why is it that I had to be born into this generation of troglodytes? Why wasn't I born into the Harlem Renaissance; wherein I could've witnessed the birth of beautiful jazz? I could have moved to Paris and wrote volumes of literature alongside Miller or Hemingway! Oh how I wish the brainless ones would all implode – leaving behind no mess to clean-up. There are a great few, however, who I wouldn't destroy; given the chance. When the mothership comes, I'm bringing my brother from another mother Chase, my main man Thomas, the boy MJ, the impeccably ingenious Miss Weigh-of-the-World, and a few others who I cannot recall right now. We could all send the napalm missiles down to Earth and watch the world burn.

…

      "You is always in the stairwell!" I nodded my head slightly and responded, "Yep", even though I should have hit her with the blues. I should have said, "Yes, I like sitting here in cold, concrete isolation because I can't stand the drivel that pours from you people's mouths. I hate all of you and if you don't get away from me within the next five seconds, I am going to rip the trachea from your tiny little neck." I never find the right words in time.
****

Have you ever looked in a mirror?
Or are you really that oblivious?
That damn fake smile you give me
I try and kill you with my eyes
I want to kill you with a knife
You are an insignificant
Low-life
Microscopic

Minuscule
Peon
Your life means nothing to me
I hope you burn in the wreckage
****

Finally, they find you dead. As you lay there, breathless and cold, you begin to wonder why you didn't kill yourself sooner. You ponder what it was that made you cling on to life for so long. Everything has become clearer in death. You never loved her, she never loved you. Years ago, you were both only in it for the sex – and then you stayed for the kids and financial stability. But now you're finally at peace – you are at home.
****

Humanity
Angry, clumsy
Killing, stealing, lying
Leader officer; thief, executioner
Aging, dying, pleading
Agonizing, pitiful
Grave
****

After all the years of misogyny and oppression, she decided that she hates all men. She took her hatred and used it to become a serial killer of men. She slaughtered human males and sewed their testicular skin into clothing items, bags, blankets; whatever the hell she could think of. I can't really blame her I suppose. She doesn't discriminate much. The only males she won't kill are gays and pre-adolescents.
****

Everyday the picture looks a little more crooked. The picture used to be perfectly level, but now it has been turned a whole 45 degrees to the right. You start to fear the tilt of the picture. You wonder if it is at all possible for the picture to become flipped an entire 180 degrees from its original position. This somewhat irrational fear never leaves you and you begin to fall apart. One day, you come completely apart and they put your remains up in a museum. The tour guide always stops at your

exhibit and says, "Now this, folks, is what happens when you can't stop obsessing over the future. No flash photography, please."
****

Lifetime of denial
Just admit it
You've been there for years now
With all those people you hate
What happened to temporary?
What happened to your band?
Your book?
Disintegrated and dissolved
Faded dreams plastered on your fantasy walls
You have folded in on yourself
So many I's
So many mes
So much hate
Hate for all the Is and the mes
****

The crushing entanglement known as human interaction; you know how it is. You try and talk to them. You manage to get a few words out – words that feel like boulders trying to move up your throat. They talk back and you can feel the mighty python constricting your airway. They continue to talk to you and soon enough, you're on your hands and knees. By this time, your face has turned completely purple, and you have lost most of the feeling in your arms and legs. So now you must speak yet again in a vain attempt to try and talk yourself out of this horrible situation. Now, with every word comes another boulder, and the python is continuously tightening its grip. At last, you drop dead. The human walks away, kids come and poke at your corpse, and you find yourself grinning. You are smiling because through it all, insanity pokes its head and you wouldn't want it any other way.
****

Sometimes my hatred makes me do things I later regret. Today I told this annoying girl how I really felt about her. She was bitching and moaning about her sucker boyfriend not kissing her on Valentines Day or some shit. Like the asshole I am, I say loudly, "Sounds like a real third-world problem." It takes a second for my words to register in that narcissistic peabrain of hers. She asks, "What did you just say?" and I repeat myself. Of course Blondie, with her forever charming and passive ways, tells me to just let the girl have her little problem – in a vain attempt to keep the peace. But by this point, my hands are trembling with rage and it is too late to reason with me. The stupid girl asks, "What did I do?" in that whiny victim tone I hate so much. So I look at her with bloodshot eyes of anger and say, "You're just fucking annoying is all." She says nothing in rebuttal, and moves further down the table from me. My anger subsides and I decide to leave, before I make my presence in ceramics any more hated.

****

Sometimes I once again feel like the only being in existence. All these humans blend in with the characters I make-up in my head. I've been ridiculing myself for these faults. I remind myself how pathetic I am, so I can improve. When I get all wrapped-up like this, I truly feel like none of you people exist.

…

I want to move far away from humanity. I want to move out to the middle of the desert, and watch the sun rise above and then fall below the sand for the rest of my life. MJ told me that he wants to kill everyone in class, except for me and a few others. I feel honored.

****

I don't give a fuck

I got all Fs

I got ten credits total my junior year

Yeah, whatever

I don't care at all

I just like to get high everyday

My parents smoke too

They don't really care about me

After I turn 18, I'll move to LA

I'll suck a few dicks

I know nothing about music

But I look good
And I'm white
So I'll make it with ease
Hey man
Don't look at me like that
I'm not braindead
"I brilliant"
****

It's loud in here. It is loud with the sound of idiotic conversation. It's cold in here, but I'm burning up on the inside – burning with hatred for my own arrogance and pompousness. Here I am, sitting next to one of the few great geniuses of my time, and he's actually trying to talk to me. Meanwhile, I'm too focused on writing in my stupid little notebook to pay him any attention. I feel hated by most of my peers, I cannot blame them. I get into these dramatic fits where I feel like a monster. I start to wonder if the people here are all actually good people and that perhaps I am the shitbag mutant. So goes the Alien Trudge.
****

"Oh boo fucking hoo. All you do is complain about your own intelligence, and your peers lack of. Stop your whining, and go out there and do something with your damn life." Having a different mind than that of my peers' hive mind is hard sometimes. I wouldn't trade my differentiation for the world, but having a mind of my own makes it hard to listen to this fellow tan man talk about how we should enslave all white people. I really just want to get out there and do something that's away from them all. I want to make this life my own; get away from all the unnecessary human interaction. I want to do something incredible, something that I could really be proud of. I've been in a state, lately, where I can't help but think of how useless it all is, but then my determination to set it all ablaze shows its face and I get out of it. This ice covered path is slippery, and I've only just begun my trudge on it, but I packed my steel cleats and I'm good to trek on for planets.
****

All of you think that I'm insane, with my ideas of foregoing government rule and living as the animals do. But is this so-called

"civilization" business really worth keeping-up? The farmers keep herding all of you animals into the slaughterhouse and you just keep rolling with it. Your social media and streaming services are selling drugs and crime to the youth but hey, that's just society for you. Pigs drive around in their little pig cars, harassing whoever they please but hey, that's just what they gotta do to keep everything nice and "civilized". You're all slaughtering each other, stop trying to hide it behind all the rainbows and unicorns. Bring the facade down.
****

Her studio apartment had become infested with cockroaches. They came in a few years ago, and she hasn't minded their presence since. The roaches mind their business, and she minds hers. When the roaches climb on the wall that she named Brick, she smiles and compliments her only friend on his indifference toward the bugs. The cockroaches and the woman have come to an agreement. The apartment is owned by no one – it is but a mere vessel meant to contain lost life forms.
****

The ladder that you will never climb. That person who you will never hold. There is always a limit to how far you will go. All those people you won't slaughter and their houses you won't burn down. Why do you set the bar so low? Why do you even feel the need to set a bar? Why is it that you have all these limitations on your life? The wife? The fucking kids? Miles Davis had three before he turned 25 and that didn't prevent him from becoming the best damn trumpet player to ever do it. You only set all those limits because you're scared. That's the difference between me and you; I left all my fear back in middle school.
****

I'm flying through the sky tonight
I'm soaring through the midnight sky at a dreamy pace
My wings are covered in black feathers
They blend in with the late night sky
I'm loving every second of this solitude
I'm drinking this isolation like black coffee
I will not sleep

Not tonight, not ever
****

A number of years ago, she was in love. She loved someone named Veronica. Veronica shared the same hatred and contempt for the world as our protagonist. The two would stand in the hallway at school and chuck rotten apples at passersby. Then one day, some psychotic motherfucker named Luke killed Veronica for no damn reason, other than that Veronica had the misfortune of being the sick sonofabitch's next-door neighbor. He cut-off Veronica's head late one night, as Veronica was sleeping. Luke brought the head to school the next day and showed it to our heroine during lunchtime. That was the very day when she came to the ultimate conclusion that nobody was worth the pain.

...

Hard trudge through thick mud. Death sentence spelled with blood-soaked letters. I want to fly away. I want an escape from this mundane life and these idiotic people. You know what I mean. You too feel like you're trapped inside the cage sometimes. You get to thinking there's no escape and you try to let out a scream, but nothing can escape your throat. Despite this, the enemy is convinced that you're happy and content. You let them think whatever it is that they need to think so that they will leave you alone.
****

C's poem
Endless nights
Empty days
Slaughter and starvation
Self mutilation
Your hands
Wrapped around
My neck
My hands
Holding onto
Your wrists
Narcissistic solipsism
Eating me whole

Sleepless nights
Worn-out days
******

Feeling like an only man in the middle of a desert tundra; surrounded by snow. My alienation runs deep. My alienation runs far and wide, high and low. You know what I mean. You're all by yourself right now, right? People make you uncomfortable, and you make them feel uncomfortable right back, don't you? That's what I thought.

…

So, how are the drugs? Are they any better where you are now? Are you high enough to touch the sky – to forget about it all yet? Do you feel like an omnipotent god among men yet? How are the kids? Do they still hate me? Do you still tell them about when I used to get drunk and beat you? We used to be the man and the woman, in the hot, apartment room. I used to beat your head against the refrigerator door, you would scream, then I would fuck you. Remember how the wise guys would take bets on if I would kill you on the night in question or not? The pigs were great. They would come and enjoy the show from time to time. Sometimes they would join in the fun and take their turns fucking you; but it was okay – so long as they didn't arrest me. Well, I guess I'd better get going now – I have a new hot animal machine waiting for me back in the car.
****

I was smoking with the boys upstairs, when I first heard about the drama. Apparently, Mary had stabbed William in the lung with her pencil, and then proceeded to dismember him. They said that Mary even ate some of Will's organs. I started going out with Mary a few days after I heard the news. What? How could I not date Mary – with all that ass she's got? About a month in, she told me that she wanted to go somewhere exotic. I booked a trip to Mexico and after telling her about it, she told me that Gualalajara just wouldn't do. I promptly dumped the greedy bitch, seeing as I had already tapped that ass by that point, and now I'm moving far away. Rest assured, I'm *never* going back to my old school.
****

Hot sun
Hot pavement
Black bike
Black shirt
Black shoes
Cold water
Cold soda
Cold lake
Cold sweat
Nice river
Nice bridge
Nice field
Nice park
Nice town
Riding hard
Riding fast
Riding slow
Riding day
Riding night
On a regular summer's day
****

Ballads:

1) Empty minds full of voices. Voices carrying disparity and loneliness. The days melt away and the nights won't end. Disturbing images are burnt into my retina and I wish to go blind. The snow has melted but the cold refuses to leave. Go smoke your pot and leave me alone.

2) They walk and I run. They hide and I paint myself neon colors. They fuck and I read. They shoot-up and I exercise. I will become the opposite of American society. I will become the opposite of all that is grimey and disgusting.

3) Venus was from the planet Venus. Ordell was from nowhere. Ordell liked Venus and her red-hot surface. He was selfishly in love with Venus's depression and alienation. Ordell never told

Venus directly how he felt; he died alone with millions of dollars in his various bank accounts, and no debt.

4) The Only Man sits on the ground – in the middle of the desert. He eats the reptiles, as they slither and crawl past. He snatches them up, one by one, and devours them raw. Whenever it rains, which isn't very often, he opens his mouth and tilts his face up to the sky, so that he may hydrate. The Only Man sits quietly, just waiting for everything to come to life. He waits for the cacti to sing and for the lizards to scream. He's waiting for the world to burst out in flames.

****

Venus does not hide behind a mask
She does not wear make-up
She obscures no pain
Venus has no vanity
She knows the ultimate truth
That she is perfect how she is
Venus has no moon to call her own
But she does not long for one
Venus is selfless
That is why she is the most beautiful planet in my eyes
****

The cold desolation reminds me of mind deterioration. So many foolish Americans with nothing better to do than to get all their beliefs from celebrities on the internet. So many of these people turn off their brains, and turn on their phones. They get their weekly mindset from the latest dicksmack on Ticktack or Chatsnap. One week it's positivity and bullshit, the next its God and damnation. But me, I'm down here in the ever-burning hole. Down here there is no HBO Max or smartphone propaganda. All that exists down here is self disgust and fire. In fact, everything in here is on fire; even me. I keep trying to put myself out with gasoline, even when water is more easily obtainable. Perhaps subconsciously, I want to keep on burning forever. Life spent burning is better than life spent living the way you are.
****

All day and all night long, she thought about it. She thought about how easy, how painless it would be. All day long at work she thought about the gun and how it could be the solution to it all. She liked to put the barrel in her mouth, just to see how it tasted. She talked to the west-facing wall, Brick, for countless hours; debating whether she should do it or not. When she slept, she dreamt of her brains being spattered against Brick. She imagined the animals coming into her apartment, and licking the blood off the floor. The rats would feast upon her rotting corpse, and the cockroaches would make it into a home. Death seemed more and more reasonable to her as the days went on. Then one day at work, she decided that when she got home, she would finally do it – she would finally kill herself. Unfortunately for her, she picked-up one of her co-worker's shifts – figuring that she might as well be useful to someone before she dies – and did not get home until ten o'clock that night. And of course, when she got home, her apartment had been broken into; and the thieves had stolen her gun.

INTERMISSION 5:

MARS' JOY

Mars always wears a smile
She is never down
Never depressed
Or so it appears
Mars is never truly alone
She has two moons
They admire her from afar
But beneath Mars' thin atmosphere
Under her almost nonexistent layer of protection
Mars is completely alone
And no matter how many machines
Or how many explorers grace her surface
She will never not be by herself
This is Mars' splendorous curse
She is never unwanted or alone
But she can never truly be with another
It is what has caused Mars' decay
Her inner solitude and thin atmosphere
Have both made her rust
But it is that rust
Which gives Mars her beauty
Her pain is her most gorgeous feature
What makes most things look old and ugly
Look used-up and thrown-out
Makes her one of the most beautiful planets of all
This is because despite her damage
Regardless of her sorrow
She finds a way to smile big
She smiles everyday
And all day
For the rest of her life

THE RAMBLING POEM II

I don't want to stop this
Whatchamacallit
"Monologuing"
I'm really starting to like it
You know,
I considered you a human once
But that was a while ago
My sister came into town today
Number Three, my dad, and I were happy to see her
We all went and visited our uncle
Reminded me how fucked-up everything is
I still don't know
Why it is that you're reading this
I don't like your kind
Humans
Pft
Feh
How weak
How pathetic
If someone told me
"You're only human"
I would take it as an insult
Sometimes
I wish I were with my own kind
But alas
They're all dead
Except for my brothers
And my father
But I digress
Oh shit
It's 2:22 AM
I started this rambling crap
At 1:43 AM

I can no longer watch
Or read anything taking place in a high school
I know that the time is approaching
Only 22 days left
Fuck
I see corpses when I dream
On occasion anyway
Once
I resurrected a corpse in a dream
It was…
Magnificent
I,
Well I can't remember exactly what I did with it
I think I kissed it,
Oh, that's right!
We were about to fuck
But I woke-up as I was getting my clothes off
Summer dreams
Ha

SUPER JESUS III

He's a pimp
A hustler
A real player
And he wants you
To send him a prayer
That's right
It's the fantastic
Super Jesus!
With sapphire blue vines
And gold around his neck that shines
Super Jesus is here!
But criminals,
Do not fear
For he does not intend on saving the day
Nor does he want to wash the decay away
Super Jesus just wants to…
Hang with his whores
Unlock forbidden doors
Drink Crystal Champagne
And have fine bitches do his luxurious mane
Bang!
Kapow!
Boom!
Oh no!
Super Jesus has been shot!
Has the world forgot?
Do we give such little thought,
Into who we shoot these days?

CHAPTER 6:
The Spring Revelations

I've told myself so many lies that I have forgotten what the truth is. I have denied myself so much of what I want that I am unable to want without guilt. I hurt myself so many times that I forgot what it feels like not to be in pain. I have long forgotten why it is that I started on this cold path. Sometimes I just want to stop this ridiculing, disciplined path and walk-on somewhere else. Sometimes all I want to do is burn-out – let myself fizzle out in peaceful tranquility like the rest of you. But I know that if I did that, I would regret it deeply. Things will get greater later, I must continue to be patient. But for how long must I keep waiting? Deep down inside myself, I know that this self-inflicted pain will never be gone for good. On and off I will continue to mutilate and deny, until I am completely numb; until I have completely forgotten who I am or why it is I came here in the first place.
****

I'm pissed-off at these microscopic fucking peons. They get on my last damn nerves with all that little sensitive, hypocritical bullshit they keep pulling. I won't go into full detail – lest I make one of these pussy motherfuckers cry – but I will say this: Fuck your controversy. These apes really think that they know me. They think that they know my every move and that they have the upper hand; but they're sorely mistaken. I'm keeping score of all this shit they're putting me through, so I can pay them back with 100% interest. The good ones will laugh, and the jackasses will cry by the time I'm through. The fakest fakes will say to me, "Ay man, yo' real good man. I was always fuckin' wit' yo' shit MAN. I always liked yo' style MAN. So, how about some bread MAN?" I'll just laugh and spit in their faces, before walking away and calling in the napalm airstrike.
****

I was walking up the street the other day, when I happened upon a guy lying on the ground, dead. He had a gun in his right hand and a piece of notebook paper in his left. There was a gaping hole going straight through his head, with a large pool of blood surrounding the wound. I grabbed the piece of notebook paper and read what was written on it.

"Well, I see you got the letter. I just couldn't take it anymore after the divorce, so I had to end it all. You're probably going to hear about the death of your mother soon – that was me.

See you in hell,

Dad"

After reading the letter, I balled it up and shoved it down his slimy throat. The so-called corpse of my father starts choking and raises up off the ground, like a zombie from a horror movie. My dad manages to spit-up the little bullshit suicide note, and then proceeds to kick me in the chest. "You lil' summabitch!" he bellows. "You tryin' to kill me? Huh, Boy? You tryin' to kill yer old man?" My "reanimated" father lights-up a cigarette, and walks away – leaving behind a trail of unused brains and cigarette ash.

****

The boys and me used to smoke on the steps of our high school. We would sit at the top of the west stairwell, right outside of Mrs. Bitch's classroom, and smoke our cheap cigarettes. Mrs. Bitch would come into the stairwell, from time to time, and yell at us and tell us to go smoke our shit somewhere else. We would always just blow smoke in her face, and she'd usually piss-off after that. The boys and me would often be sent to the office for causing disturbances like that. The principal, Ms. Sherbert, was easily bought-off with pot though – so we always evaded trouble by giving her some of the wacky tabacky.

****

I was walking down the hallway one day, when I noticed a dead body lying in my path. It laid there, rotting and festering; with maggots and worms coming out of every orifice. Flies swarmed it like a plague of locusts. My curiosity peaked, I poked the corpse with my pencil. I gave the carcass a good jab in the right side and it reanimates itself, somewhat, to a zombie-like state and says, "Hey man, what the fuck?" Startled and terrified, I run-away down the hallway. I eventually slowed back down to my normal stomp and happened upon a great, big oak tree that had somehow managed to grow out from underneath the tiles in the hallway. The tree was so tall that its branches could not be seen from inside the school. The tree's mere existence and perplexing size had transfixed me completely, so I came closer, and extended my hand to touch the tree; making sure I was not hallucinating. As my fingers come into contact with the tree, it turns into a pretty, curly-haired blonde girl; and my fingers are now in her mouth. I quickly retract my fingers as she punches me in the face and asks, "Hey man, what the fuck?" Visibly embarrassed, I once again sprint away and don't stop until I reach the twin glass doors at the end of the hallway. I exit the school, unchain my bike from the bike rack to my left, and start riding toward home. As I ride past some bushes, a pack of killer kung-fu wolf women jump out and attack me. They began to claw-off my clothes and bite off chunks of my flesh. They force me to the ground and the leader pounces on-top of me. I could at that point think of nothing else to do than to resort to violence, so I punched the leader in her snout-like nose. The leader of the killer kung-fu wolf women gets off me and the rest of the pack scurries away. The leader stands up, looks down at my bloody and battered body, and yells, "What the fuck is wrong with you?"

****

I'm done – I have been completely drained of energy and motivation. The walls lie and the ceiling crushes. The cracks are so truthful that it hurts. The ground does nothing and asks for nothing in return. Die the perilous death of falling oblivion and burn with the pain; as the decay sets-in and you wither down to a pile of ground-up bones.

****

"So I was gettin' the scam on this gurly, yeah?" says Ricardo, while pulling out a picture of the girl in question and showing it to me. The girl in the picture looked about sixteen or seventeen. She was anorexic looking, about six feet tall, with long, blonde hair down to her waist, and a gray colored crop-top and black yoga pants. I thought I recognized the girl from somewhere, but was unsure of who she was. I look away from the picture and back at Ricardo and say, "Yeah, so what?" Ricardo puts the picture back in his pocket and with much excitement he whispers, "*SO*, I got in them pants just the other night." My facial expression changes from quizzical to utter shock, as Ricardo continues, "She was a virgin see, and tighter than Tony's lips when the police come around asking questions. Anyway, after I's finished rockin' dis gurly's wurld, I come to find out later that day that she's Motzerelli's daughter! So da next day, I shot her in da head while she was blowin' my sox off and won't nobody find her corpse neither, 'cause I dumped her in da river." I grabbed Ricardo by his pencil neck and started shaking him while yelling, "Ricky you fuckin' idiot! You've signed a goddamn death contract for us all!" Later that night, all the wise guys I once knew "disappeared", and I was halfway between Kentucky and the Mexican border. It's just more shit from the mob.

****

What is true love? Does it truly exist? I hope I never find out for myself. When I think of true love, I think of two people. They meet, start going on dates, share items and experiences – they make each other happy. Then, after a while, the two get married. After the honeymoon is over, the two slowly begin to realize that they are now stuck with each other for the rest of their lives. They create or adopt a child in order to relieve some of the tension and try to rekindle what was once between each other. They divorce four months after the kid's fifth birthday. One of them takes most of the other's shit and everyone lives miserably ever after. Is that what true love means to you?

****

The stair boy sits in the stairwell that's warmest. He sits and waits for absolutely nothing. Why does Stair Boy sit and wait for nothing? I do not know and could not care less. He is a loner who doesn't want to be alone. He hates everyone and yet all he wants is some company. There is no good reason for Stair Boy to be this way. Most people want to be or try to be, but Stair Boy just is. Stair Boy is just some motherfucker sitting on the stairs. It's in his name so it's what he does. Stair Boy likes to stare a lot. He stares way out into the void, and sees beyond the physical limitations of this mere mortal world. Stair Boy sees the universe expanding and contracting like a beating heart. He sees the murderers of tomorrow in prison without bail. He can see the light at the end of the tunnel and the black void that consumes souls. Stair Boy looks angry, but he's just thinking. He's thinking of annihilation and mutilation of self. He is thinking of death corporations and African starvation. His mind is full of alienation, damnation, and her.

****

Today, Ms. Interplanetary is drunk out of her mind. She's stumbling through the halls and slurring her speech. I can hardly understand what the hell she is even saying and I fear for her somewhat. Chase told me that she gulped-down seven shots earlier this morning. If I had gulped-down seven shots earlier this morning, I would be down on the ground right now – out like a light. Shit man, it's kind of funny – in a depressing kind of way. Only 11:24 AM and Ms. Interplanetary is already shitfaced. I almost admire and respect her ability to function under such extreme conditions. You think that this is just some story I came-up with, don't you? Well, I only wish that this were just some story; I can only wish.

****

I see you, I see your pain and strife. I can see your sorrow and struggle for happiness. You pop, smoke, and drink it all away but it never really goes away. I don't care about you myself personally, but my brother Chase fucks with you and you do tell pretty funny jokes, so it is a real downer to see you like this. You're always fucked-up now, even though there's only seven days left in the school year. But, I know that this hellish place acts as a sort of escape from the real-life hell for you. I cannot help you, because I have my own shit to get together, but I do feel some level of impersonal pity for you. I can't stand to be around you for extended periods of time because your damage really brings me down. This all reminds me of the Old Dirty Bastard of the Wu Tang Clan; another brilliantly funny motherfucker cut-down too early by drugs. You don't deserve to be in such a heap, so I urge you to get out; though I know it isn't just so simple.

****

What does life mean to you?

Dani is hilarious. She was complaining about the pain she felt from being sick, so I told her I could stab her so that she could feel some real pain. We both laughed and she asked, "Why does it look like you would really enjoy stabbing me?" I then told her the truth, "Because I really would enjoy stabbing you."

…

One day, Tony told me that there are two distinct types of people. He told me, "Adal, those two different kinds of people are as follows: There are the ones who don't take shit off nobody and get down for theirs. Then there are the ones who lie down and get tooken from. Look, alls I'm tryin' ta say is that if ya can't run wit' da big dawgs, then stay on da chain." It's really funny to me now – funny that Tony of all people would have been the one to teach me this lesson. Now, I won't say much – but what I will say is that Tony should have stayed on the chain.

****

I was in a laundromat
She was too
She looked about 16 or 17
I was 23 at the time
It was bonerific
When that girl bent over
To retrieve her clothes from the dryer
It made my pants a little tighter
She had been wearing jean shorts
So short,
They were like denim underwear
I just wanted to fuck
I'm a very direct kind of guy
So I walked right up to her
And asked for her number
"Ew creep, get away from me!"
She grabs her clothes
And leaves the laundromat in a hurry
Now my heart is broken,
My dick has gone limp
So I guess it's Borax time
I'ma milk boy
And I'm dead

****

I know a girl
She's fifteen years old

She drinks forty percent alcohol shots,
Loves drugs
A friend of Ms. Interplanetary
She steals from the homeless
And loves playing Russian Roulette
I didn't think that people like her actually existed
I thought it was all just TV crap
But the girl I write of is as real as this paper

INTERMISSION 6:

THE RAMBLING POEM III – THE CLOSER

So
I've been meaning to tell you
No big rush
But that thing
The thing you really want to do with your life
Yeah, that!
You should go ahead and go do it
Like, really soon
And not to freak you out or anything,
But
Um
You're going to die someday and…
Well,
Nobody knows quite when that will be
So not to sound like a broken record but,
Go do all that shit you want to do
Even if it doesn't work out
"You're still so young!
Enjoy your high school years!"
Sorry honey
But I don't have the time for freetime

CHAPTER 7:
Dead-Man Summer

So I was riding my bike along a street that goes underneath an overpass the other day, right? Whilst underneath the overpass, I happened upon this small home made of cardboard boxes, old plastic crates, and various other pieces of trash. I call this conglomeration of garbage a home, but it was no place fit for a human to live in. No one was "home" at the moment, so I decided to stop and investigate the place – without touching anything. After stopping, I noticed a shopping cart being used as some sort of storage compartment; mostly containing old, broken toys, clothes, and things that most Americans would classify as garbage. There were quite a few articles of clothing, empty plastic and paper bags, discarded bags that once contained various snack foods, broken glass, empty soda cans and bottles, and used needles. A laundry basket served double as storage for the clothes, and as a door into the cardboard shack. Most of the clothes contained within the basket were clothes meant for small children.

****

Niles, Michigan: Buried deep beneath the ever-shifting African sands of Egypt, lies awake the ancient god of disorientation and dismay. He is god of all that does not exist, the opposite of reality. He is the god of antimatter – a god without a name. His mere existence is unknown to most, his presence is unfelt. The god of anti-matter has existed for longer than time itself. He did not create the universe, rather, the universe formed around him. This long forgotten entity lies underneath the Egyptian sands, waiting. He has always been waiting. The omnipotent un-creator himself can only wonder what it is that he is waiting for.

****

I am a parasite. I leech-off the incompetence and self-doubt of others. I am none other than: Toxo Man! I will act nice to you and treat you like the center of my universe; only so I may later benefit from the misery that I am sure to cause you. I thrive off of my own inflated ego. I only go to the mall to get digits from any girlie with black hair and fat ass thighs.

I recently got with a girlie named Katie. She drinks a lot and does plenty of drugs. She had a boyfriend when we first met – I made sure to bring an abrupt end to that relationship. She loves me, but I do not, and never will love her. Such is the way of Toxo Man, the toxicity inside us all.

******

I can still remember a time before Earth. There was mostly nothingness, aside from a few infant stars floating around the once so great void. Time was not yet a factor, so I do not know how long I wandered the infant cosmos before I met him. Even after all these millenia, I can still vividly remember our very first encounter. I was traversing the endless abyss, when out of the corner of my eye, I noticed a brilliant golden light of which the likes I had never seen before. I instinctively flew toward the light and as I drew closer, I began to make out what appeared to be another celestial being, unlike the balls of gas I had become accustomed to, but not unlike myself. Once I had gotten within arm's reach of the celestial being, he turned around; as if he had sensed my presence. He held out a small, spherical object. It was quite unlike anything I had ever seen before – being made of solid matter (much like myself) instead of being made of gas; like the not-quite-yet stars I knew so well. I reached my hand out to touch the ball, but as soon as my fingertips made contact with the sphere, it turned from brown to black and disintegrated into nothingness. My asterial counterpart was unbothered by this, and so he simply began rubbing his hands together, until another small sphere became visible. I watched as he made nine spheres, all of varying size and shape. He stacked the spheres into a pyramidal pile and held his hand out toward me. I reluctantly grabbed his hand, wary that touching his hand may cause him to disintegrate. But he did not disintegrate when our hands met, and instead, he pulled me close and we were off into the ever-expanding abyssal cosmos – beginning an epic journey only known to us as our Ancient Travels. We saw many unspeakably beautiful and horrific sights over the course of our travels. Lifeforms were scarce; hospitality was even more rare. Now, with my power and strength diminished to an almost completely useless state, I lay shrunken and defeated in the Earth's core; wishing that the God of the Sun and I could once again traverse the cosmos as we once did, all those eons ago.

******

Niles, Michigan 7:10 PM: I do not know why it is that I ride here, all I know is that I am starting to hate it. Even this park, which is in a completely different state than the hellhole, reminds me of school. For some inexplicable reason, I keep thinking that someone will come along and talk to me. I keep thinking that someone will sit-down beside me, at this picnic table, and start talking to me. Think or hope? I am pathetic.

The sun shines

It shines upon all

It discriminates against none

The sun is the ultimate power

Because

When it dies

We all die

A horrible, painful death

Frozen in a sea of hate

The St. Joseph River flows before me. The sun has begun its long descent below the horizon and the light it casts upon the river is the most beautiful, blinding hue of orange. I see the river and I picture blood in place of water. All I can see is blood tonight. Blood and gore on a gorgeous summer evening.

South Bend, Indiana 11:32 PM: I, I don't even know myself anymore. My hypocrisy is incredible. So, she sat behind me, facing the river. We start talking, fast-forward four hours and now I'm alone in my room with an empty mind full of her phone number. I can't even stand to be me right now.

****

The sun turns black

The universe turns cold

Earth splits in half

The power of the unspoken god,

Is awoken and felt throughout

All of reality

Time shudders

Existence struggles to exist

The final clocks strokes

For the final time
Anti-matter reigns supreme
Never going back
Only going forward
There is no escape
Your decay is imminent
****

Black shame
When I enter the store
As I ride down the wealthier streets
They do not see me
They can only see,
What they've seen before
The young, confused fool from last night's news
The gangster wannabe
The internet sensation
They see a black picture
Painted by a white paintbrush
I write this,
Without hatred
Without biased blame
For alas
I cannot help but understand
I cannot help but sympathize
With their ignorance
It is hard to ignore
The stupidity
In a culture so hacked-away,
That it is hardly recognizable
But I digress
It does frustrate me
However
That College Board refers to me
As a black student
To them

I am not an all-A student
I am a good, black student
They care so much about having their token students
That they don't even care
About what my proficiencies are
About what I want to do with my life
Fuck them
Fuck their stupid ass college
****

I cut it off – you know what I'm talking about. I couldn't stand to hear it constantly going on and on about this or that anymore, so I lopped it right off with a butcher knife. I wrapped it with saran wrap and then placed it in a little box. I took the box to the top of Mt. Belzoni and proceeded to throw it as far as I could. I will not be missing that thing. I wish sometimes I were born without it.
****

Riverside Trail: As the sun sets on a perfect summer evening, the BMX Gladiator blazes through the street on his bike. The BMX Gladiator never slows his roll, his wheels spinning so fast that you can't even see his spokes. Tonight, the BMX Gladiator is on an epic quest. He is on a great expedition – searching for something. The exact nature of what he is looking for cannot be described, for even the BMX Gladiator does not know what it is he's looking for. He scours the desolate, slum streets of South Bend in search of this nothing, and will not stop until his conquest is complete. The BMX Gladiator will always be looking, always riding in search of that unknown something. He will look until the day he dies.
****

Adam: "So, I asked you when and why, but what was it like?"
Carl: "Well… it was sex!"
The two both give a hardy laugh.
Carl: "I mean, I dunno. She wasn't really good at it so…
Adam: "Oh yeah."
Carl: "Choose wisely next time!"
Adam chuckles and exclaims,

Adam: "I chose a damn good question!"
Carl: "I *meant*, choose a good person; the right person."
The conversation rambles on and eventually lands upon the subject of marriage.
Adam: "I don't know, I mean, I feel like humans just aren't meant to be together until death. I don't think there's anyone who I could stand to be around for that long, you know?"
Carl points at himself.
Adam: "Well, I mean women."
Carl: "Oh. Yeah, I don't think I would ever get married either."
There is a thirty second pause.
Carl: "The one exception would probably be Ms. Interplanetary."
Adam scrambles to change the subject.
Scene.
****

I was rolling down the sidewalk on my bike the other night, when I happened upon her rotting, festering corpse. She was practically bursting at the seams with maggots. I stopped, gently leaned my bike against the wall of the closed diner on my left, and stared down at her dead body. As I stood over her filthy carcass, I said to myself aloud, "I knew the smell of death was in the air today." She suddenly reanimates and, still crawling with maggots, she says, "Oh hey Adal! I was wondering when you would show up! I was really starting to worry." We embrace and she kisses me. Tears start to form in my eyes and I find it utterly impossible to continue bearing the weight of my lie. Before she can mutter another word, I exclaim to her, "NoName, I can't do this anymore! I fantasize and criticize, victimize and dramatize every night in my dreams and nightmares and I can't take it any longer. I have not come here to be with you once more," I pulled out my walkie-talkie and continued my lament, "I have come to incinerate you." I put the walkie to my mouth and said, "Do it." Then all at once, the entire city is barraged with napalm flames and with it, burns all of my memories of yearning for something and someone who doesn't exist.
****

I was initially terrified when I first annihilated reality. The endless mass of deep, black nothingness was staggeringly petrifying. I was scared almost to the point of madness at the thought of being completely alone. That is, until I realized that my fear of total isolation was completely irrational and ignorant. I had destroyed reality because of the feeling of alienation that it had for so long left me with, but now I was the only concept left in existence. There was no longer such a thing as unity, nor togetherness and without these, there could be no alienation or isolation. So now I lie in silent tranquility; unbothered by thoughts of any of those who used to exist.

...

I had been mindlessly milling around the marketplace, when I first saw her. She was tall for a woman, at least 5' 11". She had fair skin, black hair, and a perfectly curvaceous body. She winked at me as she walked past me and out the door. I decided to chase after the goddess in the peach-colored crop-top and blue jean shorts. I exited the marketplace and found her outside of her car. Speaking in a cocky, sort of chauvinistic tone I said, "I couldn't help but stare as you gracefully pranced past me, like the primadonna you are. I cannot possibly go on another moment without your number in my phone! For now that I have laid eyes on you, I do not want to live without you by my side." She was now completely under my spell, and all she could do was giggle and blush. As I reached for her hand, she turned into dust; and so did her car. The delusions you create in your mind are just pieces of reality that you have thrown away – and sometimes that is for the better.

****

Elkhart, Indiana 1:43 PM: It is but only two days until I must once again return to the hellhole. I am currently sitting on a park bench beside my backpack full of bottled waters, and my 22" ATF. I'm already sixteen miles out from home, and I plan on going farther still. Sometimes, I wonder why it is that I ride my bike so far. Maybe it's in my blood – perhaps I'm a natural-born nomad.

The geese this year are a lot more friendly than the ones from last year. A man just told the flock to flee as he passed by, and they didn't even hiss! I've seen geese chase people just for walking two inches too close to their eggs. I have a lot of respect for geese. They never back-down from confrontation and they protect their young through thick and thin. Shit, there are humans who cannot, or simply will not do the latter. Bristol, Indiana 3:20 PM: I am now a glorious thirty miles away from home. It is at this point in my ride that I see fit to turn around and seek respite at my house. Nobody who I know can relate to the pure joy I get from riding so far. Hell, I'm willing to bet nobody from my own generation can relate to this kind of riding. While their brains and bodies deteriorate from non-use, my mind grows ever sharper and my body gains more and more strength. I've been into literature since I was in fourth grade, and I've been riding a bike since I was potty-trained. This year it was Miller and a sixty mile trek, next year it will be Hemingway and a one hundred mile adventure. I won't stop until I die.

****

I have been cast-out
I have been thrown-away
Like a defective
They banished me
To a lifetime in exile
I forage with the antelope
Then I turn-around
And hunt with the lions
I can find no respite amongst nature
Nye could I be at peace with humans
My eyes grow tired of what they see
Death and decay
My ears grow weary of what they hear
Misery and woe
My heart aches to love another
But alas
I cannot
I will not
I have come to praise the SuperChrist
He can fly
And shoot one laser for each eye

                    ADAL SMITH

And yet my calls to him go unanswered
My praise has gone unnoticed
Maybe I'm just
A rambling old man

INTERMISSION 7:

                    ADAL SMITH

SUPER JESUS IV – THE CLOSER

Flying through the sky
Soaring fast and high
A laser out of each eye
And a face to make the ladies cry
It's the return of Super Jesus!
With his new crimson colored vines
And a California smile that shines
Super Jesus is looking better than ever
He'll give your mother a heart attack
As he rolls real smooth in a black Cadillac
Super Jesus rules the game
Cowards flee at the sound of his name
And hoes drop to their knees
All so they can please
My main man Super Jesus

THE ADVENTURES OF CORPSE MAN I

Deep within the shadows
Hidden in back alleys
Perched atop high buildings
There scowls Corpse Man
Corpse Man is no vigilante
Nor is he a villain
Corpse Man is just an extraordinary man
With extraordinary abilities
He has power over death
A finite ability to manipulate time
A very supernatural being indeed
However
Corpse Man rarely uses his powers
He used to quite often
Back when he was still young
But nowadays he prefers to sit and watch
He watches the wise guys
He sees the whores on the corners
He peers down at
The woman beaters
The thieves
The molesters
The Offenders
The kidnappers
The warmongers,
And many more
Corpse man tries not to judge
He tries his damndest to be understanding
But he continuously fails
Corpse Man plays by his own rules
He will
Rape your woman
Kill your daughter

He takes drugs
Corpse Man
Christ, man

CHAPTER 8:
The Return to Hell

I cannot do
What Super Jesus can do
I have no
Divine strength
Nor do I have the ability to
Tread water and lava
Fly
Shoot lasers from my eye
I have nothing
I am just a Lowly Warrior
****

There once lived a monkey named Jojo Gunne, way back in the mid 4000s BC. Jojo was a damn fool, you see. He was the kind of boy who imitated the tall tales that the guys told at the barbershop. One day, Jojo overheard one of the wise guy Zebras talking about how he once set-up a fight between two opposing animal clans – and took bets on who would win. Hearing the old Zebra go on and on about all the money he made off the fight made foolish Jojo's eyes light-up with greed. Jojo promptly left the barbershop, in search of Leo the Lion and Ellis the Elephant; knowing that the Lions and the Elephants had a long-running beef between them. Jojo found Leo the Lion, who had been getting a drink from the nearby waterhole, an hour and a half after leaving the barbershop. When Jojo told Leo jive that Ellis the Elephant was out for Lion blood, Leo damn-near snatched Jojo's head off. Enraged, Leo hopped in his blacked-out Lincoln and barreled-down the street toward the Coconut Tree, a bar that was known for being Ellis' favorite drinking place. Of course when Leo got to the Coconut tree, Ellis was there. Jojo and a crowd of betting wise guys had gotten there a few minutes after Leo, just in time for Leo to throw the first punch; which landed right upon Ellis' solar plexus. Ellis threw a right uppercut and Jojo egged Leo on, "Go on Leo, knock 'im down! He don't outweigh you but a thousand pounds!" Ellis had a greater advantage than weight class, however, because just an hour earlier, Ellis had gotten an anonymous tip over the phone that Leo was coming for him. Ellis pulled a coconut from his overcoat and as Leo froze in shock and terror, Ellis threw the coconut right at Leo's head. The coconut went directly through Leo's skull, killing him instantly. Jojo collected his money from the wise guy Leopards, Zebras, and Kangaroos – all of whom thought that Leo, a seasoned heavyweight boxer who recently retired with the world heavyweight champion title, would have easily won the fight and had no idea that Ellis was packing heat that day. Just another music-filled story from the jungle.

****

Charismatic

High-class

Underrated and overlooked

Crazy funky and fresh

Kick-starter of rock music

Bombastic with an electric guitar

Everybody's heard his music

Reelin', rockin', rollin'

Regionally inspiring

Yahoo!

****

Pedro was walking down the east stairs, when the shooting began. He of course had previous knowledge of when the shooting was going to start. Pedro had just so happened to overhear two students discussing their plans to start their shooting earlier that day. Pedro was tired of being alive, but also wasn't ready to see hell quite yet.

...

So this is it for you, huh? Sitting in the stairwell all day, just reading some fucking book written by your beloved Rollins? Oh, I'm sorry – this one is by Slim. What the fuck ever. You know what, I despise you. Why the fuck are you allowed to sit here all day? All you do is sit and complain about all that shit that doesn't even affect you, while the rest of us have to actually go to class and just DEAL WITH IT. How is that even fair? You're a damn narcissist. I always see you walking with that shit-eating grin on your face. You really think that you're smarter than everyone in here, don't you? How fucking pretentious. So now tell me, how much longer do you think you can fake it? How much longer

can you bullshit your way up, before you fall all the way back down? I'll give you another month at best. I hope you burn in hell.
****

I want to see her bleed everytime I see her. I know this sounds bad, but it's the truth. I want to watch the crimson tears flow and hear the shrieking sirens. The complexities of her character are unimaginably interesting to me. She's brilliant and charismatic; a true visionary and great philosopher of our time – I hate her.
****

Annihilation
The final frontier
Everything eventually succumbs
To annihilation
Deterioration
So is the way of reality
****

Tiny insects gathered in thousands litter the airspace like a black cloud of loud, irritating smoke. The baffling incompetence and outright ignorance of the little bugs angers me deeply; but I do not care if they die or live – so long as I do not suffer by their hands. They know this and continue to bite at my flesh anyway. The bugs inject their so-called deadly poison into my bloodstream, in a vain attempt to kill me. But I will never die from the insects' poison. Instead, my body welcomes the foreign substance and forges it into a weapon to be used against the very bugs which gave it to me in the first place.

Like the lowly nomad I wander, forever seeking the information which the absence of plagues my mind. I want for this knowledge so much that I, unlike the lowly nomad, will crush or befriend whoever stands between me and this information. This is *my* story, *my* tale of death and destruction. I will write it how I want, despite what fourth grade teaching flunkies may have told me. Some may wonder, but others already know that this is the Death of Adal Smith.
****

I'm once again starving to death in this barren and frozen-over wasteland. If this is truly where it ends, then I shall die in hell and move on to a better hell. Perhaps I am being far too dramatic. Maybe, just maybe these are the best years of my life, and I should just be happy all of the time. Yeah, that's it! I should just let them fuck me while I put on lipstick and mascara. Yes indeed! That is what I'll do. I'll just ride on that fucking train all the way down the line.

...

My cynicism and dry sense of humor have gotten me this far, how could they let me down now? Shit, it's their way of life that has led to failure in the past. Thus, for the rest of my life, I shall see to it that everything I do in life is done my way – the only way that it should be done. I will adapt when necessary, rise above when failure presents itself, and carefully examine the advice of those who know better than me. But above all else, no matter what, everything concerning me will be done my way.

****

When most teenage boys see an attractive girl in their school, they can only dream of sleeping with her. But not the fanatical Adam Joe Andrews! AJ, as he was called by his friends, was a pimp among boys; a true man-whore of a human being! He fucked and got his dick sucked until every slut had caught his nut in her butt. With every STD in the playbook, and just the right look, AJ the fantastic had a long list of hoes like elastic. You may think it's disgusting, but it's just literature. "Not the best, not the worst, and occasionally I curse to get my point across."

****

Slick and I had just gotten back from the Big Apple. Slickback scored a few new whores while we were up there, and I made some serious paper off some of those office bassheads. Walking down the hall toward Slick's luxury apartment, we were both jiving and laughing up a storm. But when we reached the doorway and Slick unlocked and opened the door, we were met by a barrage of semiautomatic fire. Poor Slick caught several shots to the head and chest, while I was lucky enough to escape with only a grazed shoulder and shattered cheekbone. A couple of days later, I caught wind that it was Jojo and his small crew who had done the hit on Slickback and I.

Now, a few weeks later, the officials on TV are saying that the old pizza parlor on California Dr. had some sort of accidental gas explosion last night. They are finding evidence of mob activity, and signs are showing that the pizza parlor probably acted as some sort of hideout for Gunne's gang. Six bodies total were found, one of them was Jojo's. Stupid fucking monkey.

****

Mindless monkeys chattering themselves into oblivion
They know not why or what it is they speak of
They just keep on talking, endlessly.
It's a pitiful disgrace to the rest of us
We have words with meaning
Words with passion and anger and sadness
But the monkeys only say empty things
They speak obscenities of which the likes you'd never believe

****

Today, I attempted to blend in with the normal people of Earth. I walked among the people, and I found their lives to be either dull and dreary, or miserable and depressing. Even those who were rich with whatever was most important to them (mostly money and power) faced internal hardships that I wish to have no part of. I thought that I wanted to live their way, but now I know the hell that humans face. I may be Corpse Man, but at least I'm not Family Man or Poor Man, or Working, Dying, Rich, or War Man. I now prefer my somewhat repetitive divinity to their random mortality. I cannot even think of a single good reason for humans' continued existence. I do not know why anyone would want to go on living the way that they live.

****

Fuck your anime, this was a real corpse party. Well, it was more of a corpse orgy really. All of the dead and festering corpses were fucking and sucking. Guy on girl, girl on guy, guy on guy, girl on girl – anything went.

…

I asked this anorexic girl if she had any plans after school today. I'm not quite sure what the hell I was planning to do with that information, but I sure did ask her. It was in my chemistry class that the idea formulated in my head. I saw Ms. Anorexia sitting across the classroom and thought to myself, "You know what, fuck it. When class ends today, I'm going to go over and talk to her." When the bell rang, the girl was the first to exit the classroom. I followed Ol' Skin and Bones out and stopped her a couple of feet down the hall. "Hey, you have any plans for after school today?" Ms. Anorexia gave me a grin and a smirk and said in a matter-of-fact tone, "Yeah, I do." "Ok." I say and walk away, heading for my next class. As I walked away, I couldn't help but smile. I almost started laughing, in fact. For some reason, I was happy rather than upset.

****

I wish not to fuck you, but I would definitely defile your corpse. Instead of fantasies about the pretty blonde-haired girl in front of me holding my hand and prancing along the seaside, I picture her dead body covered in blood and maggots. I don't talk to many girls and when I do, I don't talk to them with hopes of them being my girlfriend, I do so so I may have another reason to criticize myself. I smile when they dislike me. I don't make friends, I make enemies. I survey the English classroom for blunt objects I could use as murder weapons, and then daydream about hitting the guy across the way with one of the many blunt objects scattered throughout the room. I imagine being the target of one of these crazy white boys with guns. I picture my own brains being spattered across the wall. I can see my skull with a gaping hole blown right through it; everyone around me is laughing hysterically. Feed me more, make me stronger. I'm high off your poison and I'm not coming down anytime soon.

****

So I was cutting myself, right? Then this, like, huge Godzilla-sized alienator starts screaming and I began to feel like I didn't want to live anymore. Ms. Interplanetary and Miss Weight-of-the-World came into the room and started making-out. I turn beet-red, and they turn toward me and hiss. Their heads turn into snakes that lunge at and sink their venomous fangs into my neck. I'm dead, but am also still alive somehow. I can only watch as they tear off my clothes and giggle while taking pictures of my naked corpse. I soon realized that I was still alive, so I left the room and made my way down the hall, toward the school exit. While riding home on my bike, I felt like just melting into the cracks of the sidewalk.

****

Power-up
Strike an ARK
Don't be afraid
Of a little spark
Weld fast
Weld slow
Burn that metal
Give us a show
The sparks will jump
The sparks will fly
You will not get high
Off the fumes
Oh no!
The steel is on fire!
Your clothes are on fire!
You're on fire!
I can smell your flesh melting
And it smells just like chicken
It's making me hungry

****

Death and decay is all around me now. I fear my quickly approaching death, only because I cannot say that I'm going to your heaven. I thought about a girl killing herself with me today. No one in particular, I just thought it would be interesting to commit a double suicide. Blood is so sexual isn't it? The crimson color, the metallic smell and taste, the way it oozes out of a wound. So fucking hot.

...

Nothing. I feel like nothing. I feel as if I do not exist, and that is not a bad thing. In fact, I'm enjoying this peaceful nothingness quite well. I don't feel the need to be something – like you are. I just want to disintegrate on this stoop I'm sitting on. I am in love with the melodic sound of the Earth's heartbeat; because it sounds like nothing. Your world is dead to me. All of you burned in the wreckage, and I am all that remains. But wait! If I am all that remains, then does that not make me something? I feel like nothing, but I am actually something. This is a complex problem of great magnitude. It is a philosophical dilemma and constant nightmare. Perhaps if I were dead, then this problem would cease to exist. But who is to say that I would not just be sent right back here? Right back to this horrible mudball.

****

"All night long. I could do this all night long." That's what he said mere moments before he came inside of Sady. Two weeks later, Sady was pregnant, and he was on the floor of his bedroom, with an extra hole in his head and a gun in his hand. When she told her dad, he got drunk, beat her, and proceeded to pass-out on the couch; while the TV blared a John Wayne movie. She tried to get an abortion – all she got was a middle finger and some asshole telling her that she was some sort of murderer. Today, Sady performs in a South Bend strip joint, and her kid has been dead for months.

****

Well, I ain't got no money to spend, nor do I have any time to waste. But let's get together and get straight. I'm a crazy lover hon. I'll rip your hair out with one hand, while I claw your eyes out with the other. Those other guys may brag and jive about how sweet they are, but I ain't no bullshitter so I'll tell you right now girl that I ain't no canned peach. I'm bitter as black coffee, but I'm sure to rock your world better and harder than any of those other cats. I'm hotter than the sun on the Fourth of July in Texas and I'm sure to make your legs shake and sweat. Well, I'll say it again: I'm a crazy lover and baby, and I think you're a little crazy too.

****

Ladies and gentlemen, I believe I have found her. I have found the sexiest woman alive. She's a critical thinker with deep and complex philosophy in her mind. She has the vocabulary of a thesaurus; so hot. English, math, history, whatever and whenever, she's your girl. She's so intoxicating when she reads. When she opens a book and her eyes start to dart back and forth across those pages, it really makes me hot. Damn, her intellect is so beautiful; too bad you will never know what I mean. You probably wouldn't even notice the things that I notice about Miss Weight-of-the-World, would you? Yeah, didn't think so.

She who rides upon her great, gold-maned horse is the one who makes me want to be a better person, almost. Her words alone are far more attractive to me than any bionic woman or social media influencer (synonyms). I yearn not for her touch, but for her company. I wish to exchange words with her for hours on end. She is the only one of those mutants I have ever met who has made me feel this way – she must be terminated.

****

Alone in the void
Wandering from soul to soul
Looking for the missing piece
Could it be you?
Or what about you?
Nope
Funny joke
Rejection hits like arthritis
It comes and goes
Eureka!
Self-mutilation is the medication!
Now addicted to the drug of distraction
Watching the blood drip off of my skin
Into the sink
Is so satisfying
Makes you want to do it again
And again
And again
Never stop
Tiger-striped with the tears of my soul
How pathetic

INTERMISSION 8:

COMMON HOUSEFLY

Pest
Annoyance
Disgusting piece of filth
A damn fly
A few of my common names
Of course, by names
I mean the terms
By which I am referred
My real name?
The one my pals used to call me,
Before they were all slaughtered?
I can't even remember
Doesn't matter anyway
You probably wouldn't understand it
It wouldn't be in human tongue
All my life,
All I've wanted is out
My buddies and I
We used to swarm the invisible barriers
In hopes of escaping to the outside
But alas
We never did
Now, I'm 648 hours old
At the end of my lifetime
I reflect on my life now
Why I never bore eggs
Why I could never escape from this hell
So many whys
Absolutely no because to answer them
This is life
And you just gotta deal with it

GOD OF DETERIORATION

They hate me
All they want to do is create
While I can only destroy
Everything I touch is obliterated
Disintegrated to nothingness
Torn apart to the smallest molecules
The other gods think I'm scum
They have exiled me
Discarded me like a piece of trash
Now, I scamper through society
Like a common rodent
I'm the rat eating at the hearts of men
You think that you're bad?
You feel like the scum of the Earth?
Try being the reason for decay
The reason for deterioration
For man's love of destruction
I have come to hate myself
I touch myself
In hopes that I too
Shall be incinerated
But alas
Deterioration cannot be deteriorated
It is the only indestructible concept
So here in the hearts of men
On top of the sun too
I sit
And I wait for everything around me
To be completely incinerated

CHAPTER 9:
Trek to the End

Okay, let's do this. So I was walking down Endless Street last Wednesday, when I saw your corpse on the ground; in front of Jovani's Pizzeria. I kicked your corpse in the ribs one good time, and it bit me! The surrounding area of the bite has started turning all sorts of colors – red, blue, black, green, and yellow. I've started to worry that I too, may turn into a corpse. Some mornings, I can feel my skin decaying. I look-down at my stomach and see an absence of muscle or fat. My ribs have started poking out far from the rest of my torso and my eyes sink further into my skull everyday. Death comes out of my mouth every time I speak, so I have to brush my teeth every hour. I suppose it is my own fault that I am becoming a corpse. I chose to fight a monster, and so it is a fitting end for me that I too must become a monster.

****

I'm on the brink of total annihilation
I can feel my bones crumbling
My flesh is melting
I am turning into nothingness
They say atoms can't be destroyed
Only displaced
Well, I'm about to disprove that
Aha!
I just thought of a new word
I will "ungenerate"
Fuck you Orwell
Yes!
I shall "ungenerate" matter
I will turn into antimatter
Wait, no
Antimatter is technically something
I'm just trying to be
Nothing

****

Shame
A deeper meaning than what appears in the dictionary
Not a clear-cut definition of the term

It could mean being wrong when you should have been right
Or it could be dropping her into the riverbank below
Or perhaps it is neither for you
Maybe for you it is selfishly lusting after someone
Or becoming obsessed with the talents of a peer
You see, shame has become meaningless to me
The word has come to mean so many things that it means nothing
Only concrete words mean something
But shame is not concrete
Shame is clay that has been molded into many different shapes
It has never had a shape of its own
****

All of those little insects out there; crawling on the walls and trying to survive in preposterously dangerous places. They all make an almost inaudible, yet satisfying crunch under my boot when I step on them. I do quite enjoy ending their insignificant lives. It humors me to think that one step of mine is all it takes to end several of their lives.

…

Sometimes, all I can do is dream of suicide. I know it's a weak way out, but the realization that it is an option really keeps me going at times like this. I feel like a selfish prick when I think of Miss Weight-of-the-World. I can't stand my weakness for her. I tried to send her a mental message that I hate her today – I wonder if she got it. I do not know how to love a person. I only know how to appreciate, tolerate, or hate. So, I guess I hate Miss Weight-of-the-World.
****

I looked at her
Those beautiful brown eyes
That gorgeous ebony-bronze hair
I looked at these qualities
And I shot her in the head
No
This still isn't a love story
I am incapable of that emotion
This is just,

How I remorse over another
It may sound dark
But it's just…
Different
Yeah
You don't get paid enough to understand
****

She stabbed me in the throat. As repetitive as it may sound to you, there is a point to my suffering. She laughed hysterically as I lied in a pool of my own blood, choking. She told me that she does not love me, rather, she loves to hate me. At night, she comes into my room while I'm asleep, and jabs me in the ribs. She water boards me some nights as well. Sometimes, she likes to spit on my shoes and piss in my face. Do not feel any pity toward me though. For it was I who raped her when she was in high school. I tore out all of her hair every month, until she learned to keep her head shaved. I hacked off her left ear with one fell swipe of my saber. When she was sleeping, I would pull out one of her teeth. When she had no teeth left, I started cutting her inner thighs with a rusty and jagged knife. I used to pluck out her eyeballs and then put them back in. So really, she's giving me mercy; I should be dead right now.

…

Nothing would change. The birds would not stop singing, nor would the cicadas stop their loud chirping. Wait, no. I must interrupt your regularly programmed lament to address the stupidity surrounding me. I had never experienced people so dense, until I entered high school. I may be in an AP class, with the so-called "smart kids", but they're just as stupid as the rest. Through my eyes, they appear as brainless mutants. The latest example: "Is it okay for us juniors to date freshmen?" "She's fourteen and you're about to be seventeen!" Do the math, in a year he might end-up being the next R Kelly. (Just, you know, without the whole pissing thing.)
****

A battle for the ages
The greatest spectacle of our time
Two gladiators

Battling head-to-head
That's what I saw that day
There were
Shards of bone
Hunks of flesh
And giant spatters of blood everywhere
The carnage could be heard for miles
As one shot lasers from his eyes
The other used giant wooden crosses as spears
The two duked it out for 53 hours
Two warriors entered the fray
One warrior prevailed
Who was it who won?
Well, it was Super Jesus of course!
With his superior strength
He was able to crush Mr. Christ's skull
With one hand,
I'm going to hell
****

Antoine did not know many things. He didn't know where he had been, where he was going, or where he was now; as a matter of fact. Of course, Antoine's ignorance caused him to wonder – though not so much ponder the "wheres" as much as he wondered about the "whys". *Why* did he talk like he did? *Why* did he walk and act like this? Antoine wondered why he thought the way he thought, and why he felt the way he felt toward others. But above all, Antoine wondered about the world itself. The "whys", the "whos", and even some "wheres". *Why* do humans worship each other? *Who* is really in charge of who? *Where* was the savior *who* is supposed to save them all? Antoine did not even know where in the hell this so-called "reality" really was. Antoine remained four inches over six feet tall and absolutely clueless for the rest of his life on Earth.
****

Ravenous mistress she is – with her head on fire, and her bones shattered beyond repair. She used to ride in on her high black horse, and made everyone before her cower in fear. She sported on her back the legendary sixteen-ring headsplitter. The blade was so big and so heavy, that no mere mortal was able to effectively wield its awesome power. With a ring for each of the sacred deaths, the sixteen ring headsplitter was at all times surrounded by an aura of soul intensity. The Mistress never actually used the sword on anyone. All it took was her unsheathing the blade, and any foe would either flee or drop-dead by its sheer magnificence. But now, with her bones crushed by the Calahoochi herself, and her head caught in the eternal flames of the Calahoochi's curse, the Mistress has been reduced to a mere shell of her former warrior self.

****

All you bitches know my name
I'm at the top of the game
I am, motha fuckin' Super Jesus!
Anytime I walk past
The hoes' panties drop real fast
At night I shoot dice
I roll all sevens real nice
I'll make your mother faint
I do things that you can't
I roll-deep in a black Cadillac
I give weak-hearted bitches a heart-attack

****

I withdrew my saber and cut her head off. As her decapitated head dropped to the floor, her body's arms crossed and her head hissed, "Well, that wasn't very nice!"

****

Her excitement for him had at that point in their relationship, waned. She did not anymore find him to be the mysterious man she once thought him to be. Mind you, she had not become tired of him quite yet, rather, she was no longer bewitched by his presence alone. Her excitement to see him everyday was now closer to the anticipation felt when receiving a small bonus at work, instead of the extreme excitement of a small child on Christmas morning. She felt this way seven months after they had started dating, at which time she was murdered.

Her organs were ripped out and their whereabouts would not be discovered for an entire week after the discovery of her corpse, which itself had not been found until approximately two days after she was eviscerated. The identity of the fiend who had killed her? Why, it was me – the villainous Emperor Hickock! Why did I do such a thing to someone who's name I did not even care to remember? I killed her because I am very depressed and lonely, and killing is the only thing that makes me feel good anymore.

****

Scraps
God weeps
The Earth is crumbling
Children are eating each other
Slaughter to survive
I bit a girl
She wasn't a fan
Started crying
So I cut my own head off
And served it to her on a platter
She vomited in disgust
I blew her brains out
****

I am Corpse Man. I do not walk amongst you, I float. If I had it my way, I would be in hell. My own mind is a real hellscape of unimaginable terror. Okay, I admit, that's a bit over-dramatic. But still, I keep thinking about all these things I did when I was younger and – and I wish I had never existed. Bee's tear-filled face haunts me still. Her screams echo in the endless chasms of my mind. I am Corpse Man, I should be in hell, man.

…

With blistering speed
Our hero flies to the rescue
To save humanity

Save it from the perils of greed and bloodlust
A truly awesome righteous man
With a masterfully crafted plan
That's right!
The war pigs he'll smite
He is
The incredible
The fantastic
Super Jesus!
He makes all the homies say "ho!"
And all the girlies wanna scream
Slicked-back hair
And caramel-colored skin
Super Jesus!
He's my kind of guy
****

They were tailing us hard, but Jefferson didn't care. He kept telling me not to worry about the rollers and just keep rocketing toward the hideout. When we got within ten miles of the spot, it became apparent that the cops weren't going anywhere, and there was something Jefferson wasn't telling me. I hysterically said, "Well J, what the fuck are we gonna do now? Them rollers are still on us hard and the hideout is just down the road! This is it man, we finally gonna get got. This car is full of stolen bread from that mark over in Chicago man! You know how much time we gonna get for this? Man-" Jefferson interrupted my panicking and said, "Man, quit ya damn whining! I gotta plan, okay? Just keep drivin' to da hideout. When we get there, I'll take care ah' da rollas, awright?" I heeded J's instructions and drove the rest of the way to the hideout. When we got there, Jefferson told me to pull into the garage. "Stay in da car, I'll be back." Jefferson got out and I watched him talk to the police officers through the rear windshield. They talked for about three minutes before J came back into the garage and opened my door. "I'ma go talk to deez rollas inside da hideout. Don't leave da car." Twenty minutes pass, and I begin to worry about Jefferson. I exit the car and peep through the small crack in one of the wooden boards that blocks-off the front window of the hideout. Inside the hideout, I see all ten cops standing in a circle around Jefferson, who's on his knees. The cops all had their pants pulled down.

****

I'm whisking myself away on this magic carpet ride of Coltrane tonight. I'm feeling mighty solipsistic, so there's no point in sparing any feelings. I'm tired of all the endless, brainless fools. I realize that they will never get better, and I used to be okay with that, but sometimes I wish I could wake-up the minds of the youth. Society has gone and decided that all of the ignorance and decadence is acceptable, but dammit – I just can't stand to be around it. If I'm going to live in this world then I want to at least make it somewhere I can enjoy living. Stop the damn buying-out. They take your money and tell you what to like, but that is not how things should be. Ah, what's the use? Nobody ever listens to the only one making any sense. "Why are you booing me? I'm right!"

****

I am Desert Man. They call me that because I only speak of the desert; for that is where I am from. They kidnapped me from my home and then tried to force me to assimilate into their human civilization. I walk human streets – always alone. I do not understand the humans, and they cannot understand me. I walk as an alien amongst them. I drift endlessly through their many places of life – holding only onto my contempt and passive hatred. Devastating is my liquid steel resolve; it runs through my veins in place of mortal blood. I am Desert Man. I come from the desert, and I am forced to walk amongst civilization, man.

…

I torture myself, therefore I am a masochist. I know that she will only use me up and throw me out, yet I continue to foolishly associate with her. I will never trust her, and she will never truly love me… This is how I view any relationship with any woman. I know now why it is that I always avoided them, men and women are poison to each other. I like women in passing, I even enjoy talking to a few of them. But no man and woman should ever get too close to each other. Ultimately, I prefer viewing females through my invisible barrier. I stare at them from across the room, and know that they will never know what I am thinking.

****

It is only with pencil and paper which I can even attempt to articulate my feelings for you. Your intellect and beauty transcends mere mortal words. I have never met someone who makes me feel the way you make me feel. You're so smart and charming. Every word you have ever spoken within earshot of me has made me want to exclaim from the top of my lungs the relatability which I feel toward you. The alienation and isolation you must feel around others must be incredible – for your thoughts and words are far from Earth. I do not pretend to understand you, but I feel as if we are two of the same. Your elegance and suave captivates my very being. I adore the way you dress and walk, the way you style your hair and even the way you carry your things. I feel like Coltrane singing Naima from his saxophone. I can only dream of conversating with you. I imagine all the things we could talk about, the places we could go. But alas, you are like a Goddess compared to me, a lowly and pitiful, mortal warrior. I could never tell you any of these things, out of fear that you would laugh at me or spit in my face. At least I can talk to you through this book. You will never see this page, and I am okay with that.

****

Tomorrow is another Monday. The first day of yet another tiresome week, filled with menial tasks and hourly suicide considerations. Another week spent lusting after the sweet relief of a knife in the dark. I do not hate my life, but I do not know if I can keep this shit up for another eighteen months. My rival is confusing. One minute, all I can see in her eyes is disgust and disdain and the next, she is showing her beautiful smile and talking as if we weren't all in hell.

…

Alien woman, alien man. They do not interact, but they compete with each other constantly. When one writes a six-page summary for a one-paragraph response question, the other starts and finishes an entire history project in a fourth of the time allotted to him, and still receives an A+. The aliens are constantly at each other's throats.

INTERMISSION 9:

SJVTC

"Eviscerator of happiness
Destroyer of soul and spirit
Come unto the Earth
And cleanse the planet of disease!"
Before long, we hear her black wings
The deadly sound of her swift decent
"Yes! Come hither our Queen o' Destruction, thoust power of endless
devastation shall deliver the Earth unto a new era of silence and
prosperity!"
Down on the congregation she swoops
She reaps from them her boon
Their lives
Soon thereafter,
Chaos ensues
Destruction and death ensue
Humanity begins to crumble
For the Calahoochi hath sworn her plague upon the Earth
Art thou scared?
Thou should be
We are surely doomed
…
Until out comes the sun
And with it,
Our savior!
He crashes down
With the force of one thousand tons
His presence is felt for miles
"It is as the prophecy has foretold! Here to combat the wicked darkness,
is the righteous light!"
Now,
With his awesome might
And superhuman abilities
Super Jesus shall extinguish the forest fire Calahoochi

Hasteful annihilation liketh a flaming arrow
Spectacular creation and passion, not unlike a soldier's bullet
The two collide
Bringing upon the end of the universe
Worlds start to crumble
Stars explode as the titans brawl
The Calahoochi cackles maniacally
The death of humanity has been assured

…
Now
A full fortnight later
The fray has ended
The final blow hath been blown
Two gods entered
None left victorious
And so Allah weeps
His lament is the only sound left
He sits atop his pile of rubble
All alone
His children are all dead
And Allah feels that He is to blame
But He acknowledges one remaining truth
Everything once created
Must be destroyed
Allah reflects upon the irony of his discovery of the truth
And he laughs
"The Prophecy hath been fulfilled
Until next time; my ever-crumbling reality."

LIAR

How to tell a good lie:

1. You must look the part. When telling a lie, make sure you appear as if you actually believe the shit coming out of your mouth. (If necessary, fool yourself into believing the lie is actually the truth.)

2. Layer the lie. Layering is an essential part of the lying process. A well told, strong lie should have some sort of "false evidence" weaved-in to validate the lie. Also, ensure to inject some truth into the lie, so that it sounds natural coming from your mouth.

3. Tailor your lie to the situation. Every lie you tell may use the same formula, but the complexity and tone must differ. Some lies require the use of emotion, such as sadness or anger, while others require monotone delivery and concrete "facts".

4. Keep it as simple as possible. To ensure a lie is believable, do not give away too much information and try not to let the lie run-on for too long. (Complexity is fine, but only when prompted by the person being lied to.) Only use information relevant toward the situation. Any and all falsified "facts" used to support the lie must be related to the given lie.

5. Keep your facts straight. This is the most difficult step for most to follow. When telling a lie, all of your "evidence" must correspond with each other, meaning none of it can conflict. Conflicting "evidence" may rouse suspicion, which in turn will cause you to appear nervous or flustered when confronted – a direct violation of step number one.

6. No anecdotes or stories, unless under extreme circumstances. Anecdotes may make you seem desperate to prove your point, and falsified information contained within one, when quickly spurted-out and then forgotten by you, can tear the entire lie apart. (Abandon this rule entirely if a story would appeal to your audience's personality.)

7. Appeal to your audience's feelings and/or ethics and morals. A good lie should be tailor-made for the person or persons it is

being told to. Examples include: using strong emotions when telling the lie to an emotional person, expressing distaste toward a certain group, company, or person when lying to a strongly opinionated person, and appealing to an authority figure's sense of morals and/or obedience of all rules.

8. Take big gambles, in order to gain big rewards. All lies have risks associated with them, but the best payoffs come from beautifully executed lies, filled with complexities – that will ultimately rob someone of their free will.

What you just read may leave you with a sense of disgust, or perhaps now you feel dirty. Perhaps I no longer have the credibility from you that I may have once had. But before closing this book and putting it back on the shelf, without even reading the final chapter, consider this: Everything I just wrote, I learned in English class. A well-written, argumentative essay and a well-spoken, strong lie are far more similar than you may think. The rhetorical situation, being taught to us as early as ninth and tenth grade, revolves around several basic concepts. (At least, I have only picked-up on this many.)

1. Have a strong thesis.
2. Be evidence-based.
3. Craft your argument for the audience.
4. Don't use words foreign to the general public.
5. Only use topic-relevant evidence.
6. Keep anecdotes to a minimum.
7. Appeal to the audience's feelings.

I hope my intentions are not lost on you. America is built on lies, we even use them to remodel. "I don't really mind if it's over your head, because the job of resurrectors is to wake-up the dead."

THE ADVENTURES OF CORPSE MAN II

I am Corpse Man
I possess powers over death
My mind is a festering heep of brain matter
My body is a black and blue mass of long-dead cellulose
I am forever decomposing…
I find it difficult not to…
Judge humanity
But your society baffles me
All that time you waste
Doing nothing
Killing
Stealing
Fucking
How do you continue to exist on this planet?
But I digress…
As a corpse
I am a nature lover
Though most of what I enjoy consists of plants
Plants do not consume
In the way which animals consume
They get their fix from pure sunlight
Plants do not make unnecessary noise
I wish that I were a plant…
Sometimes I wonder
What has made me this way?
Why must I be Corpse Man,
Instead of Super Jesus?
Or the God of Disintegration?
Or the god of antimatter?
I can imagine in vivid detail
My exploits as a flying pimp with laser vision
Or the time I could spend thinking
Whilst underneath the Egyptian sands

But alas,
I was born to be a corpse
Brought into the world to die
But never meant to live

CHAPTER 10:
The Tenth Chamber – End of the Beginning

The wrap-up
The end
It's finally going to be over
What an experience
What a show
What a ride
What a place that was
This is
Truly the end
You're going to like it
Trust me
It's something,
Something to die for
****

A word from Super Jesus:

I do not know what Corpse Man's big deal is. He's such a fucking moron sometimes. He gets into these philosophically driven states of depression, where all he can do is look at all the negative parts of life. First of all, the man is immortal. He literally cannot die or be harmed. I mean, he's not exactly the best looker – with his unusually dark and decaying skin that's purple in some areas – but he doesn't need to look good; the guy hates people! Shit man, he also has unspeakable abilities. Can you even begin to comprehend what it means to command any and all death (except for your own)? You could vanquish any enemy without even lifting a pinkie! Hell, I'm only a lowly pimp. I can't murder on command – I have to at least lift my right arm. That damn Corpse Man, what a guy.
****

I'll spit mad game at your hoe
Turn her out in the hallway
Tell that bitch to get me my dough
I got three girls in my stable
Tracy, Macy
And a girl named Mable
These pussyless suckas are addicted to my whores like crack

They spend mad scrilla
Just for a little smack
I learned this life from the greatest
It was Super Jesus who pulled my coat
Now he's bitchless
And I feel like the goat
****

I have advanced far beyond mere mortal intellect. The thoughts in my head are the many archaic thoughts of the universe. I walk alone because that is how I am meant to be. "Some people are better off alone.", and I am one of those people. I am rapidly advancing and improving myself because any faults within my character are pure weaknesses of my soul. I do not trust any of them, and I am stronger because of it. I have more weakness to eviscerate. I will cleanse myself until I am bare. I may not be Super Jesus, but I am the one and only, Corpse Man.
****

I want to show her The World. I used to be too immature to admit it, but now I must reveal the truth; I want to show Miss Weight-of-the-World The World. And I am not referring to that bullshit, fabricated romance world that Hollywood shows you in movies. I want to show her *the* world; *my* world. My world is one in which everything is beautiful; because everything is perfectly imperfect. From the ever-moving St. Joe River, all the way to the slums of South Bend. All aspects of life have meaning. Everything from the gorgeous robin in the snow-covered tree, to the tiny, unidentified insect crawling on the classroom ceiling. The rats crawling in the sewers are just as magnificent to me as the little turtles whom bask in the summertime sun on the riverside in my world. In my world, they cannot touch me. They cannot speak to me, hurt me, or corrupt me. In my world, I am who I am; and she can be who she is. I want to show her what I see when I ride my bike, what I see when I write, when I read, even what I see when I sleep. I want her to understand me, even though I sometimes struggle to understand myself. I want her to know what I know because maybe then, we could at least be friends. But alas, it was I who chose this cold path. I have long forsaken their way, and cannot turn back now. I tell myself that this is for the best, but struggle to believe in my own words.

****

It was 6:13 PM on New Year's Eve, and 2023 was just shy of six hours away. The temperature was above average, for the midwest anyway, sitting at about forty degrees fahrenheit. I cruised my maroon-colored Chevy Silverado down the road, en route to my brother's house. He was throwing a party and though I was usually not a fan of such things, I decided going would be better than moping around the house all night. Besides, it was time to move on from the divorce – and maybe find a New Year's hookup.

I was bringing the drinks – orange sodas, Sprites, root beers, and Pepsis. My youngest son was staying the night over at one of his friend's houses, leaving only my second oldest to tag along. We got to the party around 6:20 PM. My son and I were among the first to arrive, and yet the music was already deafening. Jr. couldn't stand loud music, so it did not surprise or anger me when he asked to be taken home after being there for only half an hour. I took him back, and returned to the party around 7:30 PM.

Nothing of much importance happened until around 9:30 PM, when my sister-in-law's friends got to the party. I can't remember their names, but for your convenience, I will number them. Number One was a tall, quiet, ebony-colored woman with a small permed afro, dyed a spectacular red and gold. The color was surprisingly subtle, but absolutely gorgeous. She wore a sexy, skin-tight dress, and knee-high, black leather boots. And to top it all off, she had some of the biggest titties I've ever seen. She was *definitely* my type.

Number Two was still tall for a woman, but shorter than Number One (who was about six feet tall). The only thing I can vividly recall about Number Two are her somewhat impressive breasts. Number Three was completely unremarkable, and was perhaps not worth mentioning.

So as the night progresses, the game-plan becomes this: Set George (me) up with Number One. With much encouragement from my brother, Number One goes ahead and sits down on the couch, right beside the chair I was sitting on. Now, I must admit, it had not been since the times of dinosaurs roaming the land, and cassettes being used as an ideal way of listening to music that I had tried talking to a woman. My game was rusty, and I was nervous. I needed not worry, however, because Number One would not even look my way, telling me that she had no interest in a recently divorced bachelor with two remaining sons at home.

At one point, Number One's phone began to ring and almost as soon as she answered, an argument ensued. After a few minutes of arguing on the phone, Number One hangs-up and begins arguing with Number Two – who was supposed to give Number One a ride home. They ended-up taking the feud outside and after a few more minutes, I'm prompted by my brother's wife to go outside as well. My brother and I both go outside, and watch as a quickly approaching catfight begins. Before things can get too ugly, my brother suggests that I, the ever so handsome and single George, take Number One home, in place of Number Two.

I wanted to high-five my brother right there and then, but I managed to keep my cool. The thoughts that went through my head in that moment are as follows: "Aw hell yeah! Now, I can break the ice between me and this woman, and then maybe…" So I play it cool, and reluctantly agree to take the woman home. But of course, as soon as the chance is given to me, it is taken away. The woman is taken home by someone else, and I am left at my brother's house, with all the drunken undesirables. I left the party around 11:05 PM, and got home around 11:20 PM. I told my son of my exploits, and then proceeded to the shower. So much for a New Year's hookup.

****

I am always in an attempt to try and upstage, outshow, and undermine her in any academic way I can think of. I do this, knowing fully well that I can never surpass her. I cannot act for shit, while she has been in multiple plays and productions. I do not have a single musical bone in my body, while she has one of the most intoxicating singing voices I have ever heard. I refuse to participate in a single extracurricular, for my disdain for this hell is too great, and yet she participates in as much as inhumanly possible. I attempt to surpass her in hopes of becoming a better person, but I know that will never happen. Oh Miss

Weight-of-the-World, you will never hear these thoughts of mine – but somehow – I feel like you already know.
****

I was rolling a smooth 55mph down Cleveland, with Coltrane and Sonny Clark oozing out of the speakers around me. I was feeling good driving my black Cadillac through the starless, black, January night. My Carhart coat was fitting just right, and my wavy, permed-straight hair was laying perfectly still atop my head, like a still life painting of a brown ocean. My mind raced with temptation and foolish thoughts of a teenage boy with his own car. In the back of my head, of course, was Miss Weight-of-the-World. All of my previous thoughts were erased from my brain, however, when I glanced at my speedometer, and then at a nearby speed limit sign with a number 40 on it. Paranoid of being pulled-over and shot on the very dark, very desolate late-night street, I reduced my speed all the way down to 40mph; and kept it that way all the way home. The intermission from my current overworked and overstressed state did not last long, as I tossed and turned myself into turbulent, nightmare-filled sleep around 11:30 PM. Now it's 3:02 AM, and I'm sitting in my easy chair, thinking of things that'd make you laugh.
****

The following was inspired by and is dedicated to my incredible friend, Thomas Glover:

These pathetic imbeciles can all go to hell. They are all intrusive NPCs in this game of life. I hate being around their brainless speech all day. Of course, I would never say any of this aloud – I aim to avoid any and all conflict. I just can't understand their pitiful complacency. I hate their strange obsession with rap music as well. These complaints only apply to my own generation, however. As for my opinion of my elders, I think that they are all complete jackasses. They patronize me because they think, for some reason, that they're above my level intellectually. They shove pills down my throat to try and slow my brain down. They say I have some issue paying attention; when in reality, my thought processes so far transcend theirs that everything they say goes right past me. I know that nothing they say is of value to me, so I cannot and will

not listen to any of their drivel. My mind can focus on multiple tasks all at one time, and perhaps they know that deep-down and fear me because of it.
****

I wish to rape your woman, shove that fucking Starbucks down your teenage daughter's throat, and crumble your entire economy in one fell swoop. I want to, no; I *need* to wipe-out the human race. If only you were all just a hive of bees in my attic, then I could exterminate you with ease. My hatred for you is a passion that drives me to continue to exist.

...

"Sorry Tim, but you got another three years before you can retire. That is, unless you don't want your retirement benefits or pension?" Over thirty goddamn years and I still can't retire, so I may enjoy what few active years I still have left. They don't even pretend to give a fuck about ol' Appleby. They're so desperate for teachers, that they don't want to let go of any hapless sucker they already have in their grasp. I fear that I'm not cut-out for this teaching shit anymore. I feel that everyday I am failing my students more and more. You may wonder what this is, but you would never guess that this is: The Problem with Appleby.
****

I cannot figure myself out. I hate so much, and love even more. My hatred is only equivalent to a fraction of my love for music, literature, and the world I find away from people. I love the sun and all the little birds flying underneath it. I love the animals in the wilderness, and all of the little plants they eat. The rivers, streams, lakes, ponds, oceans, even the man made reservoirs are more beautiful than any superficial supermodel to me. I fucking hate men, women, Starbucks, Ticktok, Chatsnap, Fakebook, Instantfuck – the list goes on. The quantity of my hate is great but the quality of my love for the things I actually care about will always be far better than that of my hate.
****

My biggest problem, I have found, is my need to be number one. For my whole life, it seems, I have been the second in line. I've always been Little Adal, the second grandchild, number two clone; never first.

It seems like my whole childhood has been a series of people telling me that I'm just like someone older than me. "You're just like your sister." "You're just like your father." I'm always the second choice. "I would have your dad fix this, but…" "Did you learn how to do that from your dad?" Almost nobody I care about has treated me as an original. The only one, off the top of my head, who did treat me as an original is the whole reason you are reading this book. I feel like a fucking repeat, a damn cliche of my own life. I am Adal Smith III – I am an original. There has never been another mother fucker like me, and there never will be again. I am the first, the last, and the only.
****

The year is 1975. Some of my family is over at the house, and my siblings and I are playing outside. The sun has gone to bed and the moon and stars polka-dot the sky. The early night air is cooling, yet it still retains some of the heat from the July sun. Ralph, John, and I were catching toads, playing tag, and jumping as high as we could – just trying to touch the moon. Being wild, young boys, we were constantly going in and out of the house.

All the adults were talking amongst themselves in the dining room, and were paying us three mischievous brothers no attention. At one point in the night, we got into our mother's purse and within the endless series of folds and pockets contained a small, pink, six-round revolver. This was truly the highlight of our night.

Bashful John was the first to take the gun and try to pull the trigger; no luck. Then Ralph, being a year older than John, attempted to pull the trigger – still no luck. They took turns trying to pull that trigger in the house for a full minute before I got the idea to take the gun outside. I figured since we could not reach the moon by jumping, then maybe we could shoot it down.

The next twenty minutes were spent outside, trying to shoot down the moon. "I wanna try shootin' the gun, Ralphie!" I pleaded. "I'm the oldest, I should be the one with gun!" Ralph looks at me with an expression of smug satisfaction and says, "I the one who found the gun in the purse, so I gets to shoot it." Then John butts-in, "No you didn't! I's the one who found the gun in da purse!" We argued about the gun and who should be allowed to shoot it until dad shouts out the back door, "Boys! It's time to come inside!"

The revolver falls into my hands, so I conceal it underneath my shirt, before following Ralph and John into the house. We went to the living room, while the adults stayed sitting around the table in the adjoining dining room. Since nobody was watching, I pull-out the gun and tried to shoot it. I grip the handle with both of my tiny, six year old hands and, aiming in no particular direction, I successfully pull the trigger.

The revolver goes off and a bullet shatters the punch bowl in the dining room, barely missing my aunt. I remember thinking that I was in for the biggest whooping of my life. But there was no whooping, no yelling or cursing. The adults were just relieved to see that nobody had gotten hurt.

****

When I walk into the saloon, everything stops. In my wake, all murmuring, fighting, and drinking ceases. The guy in the corner lights-up a cigarette and starts strumming my theme on his guitar. I order a root beer, and am met with the end of a double barrel shotgun. "This shit again?" I wonder aloud as I draw my sword and cut the bartender's head off. I then jump over the counter, pour myself a big mug of root beer, gulp-down the half suds half liquid glass in one swig, and leave the saloon. I proceed to mount my horse and off into the sunset I ride. As I ride, a starry night falls down upon the horizon, so I set-up camp near a giant boulder. The campfire light shines beautiful orange incandescence, and I hear the coyote call. By day I run with the buffalo, by evening I drink at foreign saloons, and by night I rest by campfire light – surrounded by nothing but sand. Oh yes, the cowboy life is the life for me.

****

I had just left welding class, and was walking down the semi-desolate hallways of my school when, out the corner of my eye, I spotted some girl I faintly recognized (I'll call her AlienX). She was wearing a loose-fitting, thin, green sweater and khaki cargo shorts. She looked so unimaginably beautiful walking down the hallway beside her brother,

(I'll call him AlienY). Her shimmering, curly, dirty blonde hair, the bright incandescence of her dead pine needle colored eyes: AlienX was looking like a five foot six inch package of perfect, prepossessing allure. Within mere seconds of spotting her, I realized that I was dreaming. At that moment, I ran over to AlienX. I pulled her close and AlienY disappeared. AlienX's outfit all-of-a-sudden changed to a rather revealing white tank top, beneath an unzipped black sweatshirt and black leggings. I grab the hem of her tank top, and pull it up to her chin, revealing her small breasts. I am transfixed, perplexed, and aroused – so I begin to suck her perfectly pink nipples. At the same time, I reach my hand down into her leggings and start trying to finger her. I remember her being so small and tight that I could barely fit my index and middle fingers in. Finally, I lay her out on her back, on the floor, pull her pants down, and start fervently sucking and licking her palace of desire. There is a lapse in time, and I am once again walking down the hallway. Yet again, I see AlienX. She was now the spitting image of a different girl I used to know, complete with the other girl's iconic dark green sweater, tight blue jeans, straight, black hair, and almost black irises. She smiled a sly grin and waved as we crossed paths, saying softly, "Sad sad sad."
****

She wanted someone to love, *he* didn't give a fuck. She kept flirting with him and he eventually took her out to the movies. His motivation? He doesn't even know. She was not the girl he wanted, but she was the one who spoke to him first. She started to fall for him completely, *he* couldn't care less. On the second date, she asked, "You ever had a girlfriend before?" She wanted him to say something like, "No, but maybe you could be the first?" But *he* didn't give a fuck. He said no and left it at that. By the third date, it was over. Her love was still there, but his inability to take other's feelings into consideration was too strong. After the third date, they did not speak again. He avoided her at school, *she* wanted nothing more than for him to acknowledge her feelings. *Her* heart was broken – *his* heart was closed-off. So goes the so-called "love life" of an alien.
****

She's the most beautiful girl I've ever seen, and she lives across the ocean. She has the most mesmerizing, curly blonde hair I've ever seen. Her eyes are like precious gems, they twinkle and glow in the sunlight. I yearn for her company. At night, I dream of endless scenarios in which we could meet. She's brilliant in every way. She's a philosophical thinker with a sense of humor. A true genius. I know that she would not like me, if we were ever to meet. She is not Miss Weight-of-the-World, she is yet another alien. (They really ought to stop sending us down here.)

****

The following society-shattering ideas are not from my own mind – for they are the many futuristic thoughts of society. These are ingenious philosophies; words straight from the mouth of my brother-from-another-mother Chase Ellsworth! One of the few, great philosophers of our time!

1. "Women deserve less."
2. "You're black! And black people don't have any rights."
3. "There's no reason for you to wear them tight ass pants!"
4. "Get gud."
5. "To say the black, become the black."
6. "If her weight's in quadruple digits she deserves an orbit, not attention."

These words of wisdom may be lost on you, but I assure you; these are philosophies that will help you to better understand the world in which you live.

****

They do not see
They do not hear
They cannot understand
He's thrown into the water
And told to swim
Proper instruction
Was not delivered
All Fs?
What was to be expected?

If they actually
Took the time
Listened to his philosophies on life
Then they might understand
But they do not care
Prayed on his downfall
Then blamed him for the failure
My best friend
This generation's greatest philosopher and innovator
"Unmotivated"
"Lazy"
"Stupid"
But never genius
****

At the end of his nomadic journey, the Lowly Warrior finally realized his true power. He sheaths his saber for the final time, for the blade is not one's true strength. The Lowly Warrior discovered his previously undiscovered power of control over fate and with it, his entire Universe. He could bend the will of events around him. The Lowly Warrior never again walked alone; for the Universe was always with him. The Lowly Warrior found sanctum and respite in nature. You may think the Lowly Warrior's power to be unnatural, but it is a perfectly normal power. The power to craft our own destinies is with us always, even when it seems like it's not. Trust in the Universe, and take the chances given to you. If no chances appear, create your own opportunities.
****

She was smart, but don't tell her about her brilliance. All they ever talked about was how smart she was, and how she managed to understand things that nobody else could possibly comprehend. She was one of the "Wonder Twins". She hated that nickname. Everything academic came natural to her, or so they thought. Everyone always had a question about an assignment or a test. And though she did not always have an answer, she always had to be right. Resentment and jealousy around her constantly. Glad it happened to someone else for a change.

...

She is a silent bomb, but don't tell her that. Whether she is truly aware of how transcendent her inner strength is is completely irrelevant, because she is too shy and afraid to show it to the world anyway. Society is a ruthless place, in which the loudest dog barking gets the bone, and she is incapable of so much as a whimper. She is a priceless jewel covered in thick soot. She is a Miles Davis record with no player. Sometimes, I do not want to live in such a world as this; a world in which gold-flake calcium is so sought-after, while nobody takes the time to dig for buried Jade and diamonds.

****

It was just another day at school, or so it seemed. My long-time buddy Powell and I were sitting in the back of the classroom, just talking shit and laughing at the morons around us. Powell was great in stature, standing at about 6' 2". He was dark as midnight, and built like a brick wall. As our conversation died-down, my thoughts began to wander and so I looked-over at AlienX. I started day-dreaming of holding her in my arms, when Powell noticed my transfixation. He asked me, "Ay yo man; you like that little blonde shorty over there?" I admittedly nod my head, and Powell gets up out of his seat. He went over to AlienX, and began talking to her. As I watch them talk from across the room, AlienX's eyes dart over toward me, and I look away. Powell returns after a minute and says, "Great news man! That shorty digs you too! I gave her your digits, here are hers." As my long-time friend hands me a piece of paper with AlienX's phone number on it, my phone dings. Surely enough – almost as if this were some sort of made-up story – it was AlienX texting me. I walk over to AlienX and the next thing I know, we are both drawing on the chalkboard, and I'm awkwardly trying to make AlienX laugh at my jokes. I woke-up that morning, knowing that will never happen. Damn my pitiful humanity.

****

He tagged MF before his name
Because he was a real mother fucker
Sporting all black in the summertime
He wrote with metal fingers

Because his style was rugged and rusty
Never could flow quite like water
But chose to speak poems all the same
He carried on his back everything he owned
Because he only gambled for all or nothing
The philosophy of Davis
Concise head-splitting words like Wu-Tang
A dangerous foe, take heed
But an invaluable ally, indeed
****

Fueled by Johnny "Guitar" Watson funky vibes, the god of antimatter finally decided to walk among the people. What he saw, however, shocked him. Decadence ran rampant through the streets. He witnessed the poorest of people hustling off each other, while the richest stuck-together and stole from the poor. He saw beautiful women on the corners – selling themselves for low self-esteem pimps in flashy suits and wild perms. The god of antimatter was awestruck with grief, so he left the Earth forever; now and forever traveling the cosmos in search of something that is not there.
****

I stand firm
With an old wooden pencil in my hand
A disciple of the Lowly Warrior Clan
Now turned leader,
No longer shackled by the opposition
No longer going with the flow
Carving a trail to freedom
Hoping other chained minds will follow
Distractions are aplenty
Many try and lead me astray
College scouts tell me I need their knowledge
When they don't even have knowledge of themselves
The welding creed calls out to me
Tempting me with "good insurance" and "job stability"
Bodacious women try and get in my way

But lust turned love can wait until I'm dead
My sword continuously sharpens
Its edge derives from those who fall below me
The carbon in its blade is from those who rise above me
Better watch-out decadence
It isn't safe anymore
****

Rollin' down the street
In an old school, big body Caddy
All the ladies callin' him daddy
You already know who it is!
It's the one and only, Super Jesus!
Rockin' a shag haircut so fly
Ain't no honeys passin' him by
S is for self, and savior
And my man SJ fits the behavior
****

I was walking down the barren, desert wasteland of my heart, when I saw you. The wind was tossing the sand around me into the air and yet, I could see you with more clarity than even my glasses could offer. I came up to you and offered these words, "I do not pretend to know what it is like to trust someone other than myself. I do not pretend to have melted the steel-plate armor around my heart, or have destroyed the walls around my soul. I do know, however, that all I can think of most nights is you. So now I pose this question to you: Will you please enter into my life? Because all I want right now is to learn all about yours." Your answer did not shock me, nor did it fill my eyes with tears – but it did finally give me the closure I had been looking for.
****

I am the one who moves like the wind. I can flow like water, yet you cannot move me because I am also like a mountain. I bend like rays of light, so that no matter what stands in my path, I can continue on forward.

...

Who, me? Oh yes officer, I'm the one who almost bashed that man's head in for flipping me off. I used to be really fucked-up, actually, I still am. But back in the days on the road of Ida, I used to be prone to violence. I used to throw chairs and tables at motherfuckers, just for saying the wrong thing to me. I've yelled at the top of my lungs so many times that I've developed this small croak in my voice that you can hear when I talk quietly. It's the sad truth that an accomplishment of mine is that I haven't thrown so much as a three-hole-punch at anyone for almost four years now. I remember in eighth grade, I put a kid in a headlock and repeatedly punched him in the face. I would've probably kept going until my arm gave-out, had it not been for the nearby police officer. What did he do to me? He slid my Nintendo across the cafeteria floor. (It was not broken, nor damaged.) For that offense, I was suspended for a week. My mother would take me to all these stick-up-the-ass doctors who would try and shove pills down my throat and put labels on me. "Autistic", "on the spectrum", "asburgeres", "tourettes"; all of that Yale psychology shit. They couldn't just simply say, "We don't really know why he acts the way he does" so they hit me with every label in the book. All I really needed was an outlet to vent my frustration at the world – but they yelled at me when I tried to do that too. In fourth grade, I was supposed to make-up a restaurant, and write a story about it. I, being the ever-innovative nine year old I was, decided to write a perfectly normal sounding story about a burger shack. The "innovative" part of the story was at the ending; where I revealed that the burger meat was made from the customers – who never did leave the burger shack. I thought that it was a cool twist ending, but my teacher did not. Mr. Stick-up-the-Ass said it "set-off red flags". That was the first time, but not the last, that I had ever heard that term being used. I didn't even know what he meant, other than that I couldn't write what I wanted anymore. It's fucked-up that it went right over that guy's head that a fourth-grader wrote a story with not only a twist ending, but also the use of allusion and foreshadowing. I suppose I shouldn't complain about him too much; he is part of the reason I chose to write this book. Spite is a very strong motivator.
****

I was drunk, yet again. My sobriety had been carried off, far away by my obsessive love's swift action. As I stumbled through the halls that day, I saw her – the *Mademoiselle* herself! In a drunken spur, I raced toward her. (Well, it was really more of a fast hobble.) I placed my left fingertips over my heart, and accentuated the perfectly round fingernails on my right hand, when I flung my right arm toward the sky. I looked directly into her incredible eyes and slurred joyfully, "*Bonjour, Mademoiselle Chasse!* Pardon my French, but I am drunk off my love for you; that love which has made my heart yearn and burn for you for many months now. I understand that you must focus all of your time on scholarly things – as do I – but I must truly request that you requit my love! All you must admit is your undying love for me, *Manquer Chasse*, and I will leave you alone, until you are ready to give me your hand in marriage." Sadly, the *Mademoiselle* did not find me charming, or even amusing, and slapped me across the face before running down the hall from me screaming, "*Pervers, pervers!*"

****

Jessy was a race car driver. When she got in that minivan of hers, that speedometer never dropped below eighty. She ran red lights, police cars, sports cars; nothing and nobody could outrun Jessy the racecar driver. I raced Jessy once. It was a late summer's night. The time was approximately midnight, and I was on my way home from ya mama's house. The streets were desolate, spare for one car other than my own – Jessy's brown minivan. I was coasting in the fast lane, when she passed me on the right – middle finger held high and out the window. When I saw that, I thought to myself, "There is just no way that I, the great Adal Smith, driving my beloved '99 Deville, will allow a minivan to pass me!" So I stomped the gas pedal, and boomed the Caddy down the road after her. I only passed Jessy for a brief second, however, before I heard the sirens and saw the high-beams. I pull over, and when the police officer gets to my window, he shoots me in the head twice.

****

She was lost – lost and confused in a world she couldn't understand. Suicide had not lent itself to her, so she wandered endlessly and aimlessly through life. Anointed in literature since birth, she had a certain philosophical charm about her that night, as she walked through the streets of South Bend, looking for yet another someone that was not there. Whilst crossing-over the Old Darden Bridge, her eyes caught a glimpse of what she thought was a man in the river below. She peered over the edge of the bridge and sure enough – there was a man, with eyes gray as concrete, lying underneath the water. Not knowing what else to do, she tried speaking to the man underwater, asking what he was doing all the way down there. Bubbles arose from the river, but the sound of the man's voice had been muffled and scattered beyond comprehension. Our heroine feels compelled to try and pull the man up out of his watery tomb. She leaves the bridge for the night, and comes back the next day with a one hundred foot chain she'd bought from Menards earlier that morning. She lowers the chain down to the bottom of the river, and the concrete eyes man weakly grasps it. She pulls him up and he thanks her. "Thanks for saving me," he says. "I've been under this bridge for over a year now and was sure that I would soon be reduced to nothing but dirt." She looks at him inquiringly and he tells her how he even got to be under the St. Joe River in the first place. "I used to love a girl; but that was a long time ago. Her name is unimportant, but she is the one who pushed me into those rushing waters below. Since then, I have had a long time to decide that no person is worth the pain. Sorry you had to waste your time saving someone like me." Tears well-up in our heroine's eyes, as she begins to reminisce about Veronica inside her head. Without thinking, she pushed the concrete eyes man back off the bridge. The concrete eyes man falls right back where he had fallen before. Right back where he belongs. Right where I belong.

****

The white moon is full and sits as the beautiful magnum-opus of the sky. I pull two cigarettes from the pack in my breast pocket – one for me, and another for her. She kindly turns my cigarette offer down, because she is too awe-inspiringly gorgeous to smoke. I roll-down the windows of my Pinto as I light-up my death stick and then turn to my love saying, "The moon is big and bright tonight – much like you except, you're always like this." She kisses my cheek softly and I caress her shoulder-length brown hair. Napalm, atomic bomb, teenage mom and my darling. These all become one tonight as her and I embrace under the moonlight. Star-filled sky and a teary eye on my bare chest is what I call perfection. My entire life has led to this point; this time of tranquility and romance. We exit the car and stand together on the fertile green foliage. On this peak, in the desolate woods, we hold each other close. The world begins to crumble underneath our naked feet and we tighten our grip on each other. The forest starts to engulf itself in flames, and we lock lips. The end of the world as we know it is here, but we do not fret. Passion, warmth, love, kindness and unity. We are here at the end of the world, together, so we cannot fear. Death is only a happening, as youth is only fleeting. Houses crumble, monuments shatter, people die but our spirits go on. Eternity is the absolute because nothing else lasts forever.

****

The Lowly Warrior stood amongst the flame-licked grass – sword in his right hand, remorseful paint brush in his left. In front of him stood a canvas painted with the blood of dead soldiers. Innocents lost to a war fought over petty material objects. The canvas depicted the bloody scene in which the Lowly Warrior played a key role. He could still hear their screams; their pleas for mercy as they were all wiped from the Earth. With every brush stroke, every single red streak across the canvas, brought forth flooding memories of all the faces of those who fought valiant in a battle they did not fully understand. They fought for honor alone, something that the Lowly Warrior had long forgotten. As the sun began to set and the evening winds blew the stench of burnt flesh directly into his nostrils, the Lowly Warrior thought about the true victims of this war – the wives and children that many of these men had left behind, in order to lay their leader's claim to superfluous gains. Then images of the crying mothers of the youngest of their fleet made their way into the Lowly Warrior's mind. The moon began to shine as the Lowly Warrior plunged his saber into the gun powder-hardened ground. He kept the paintbrush however, as he walked away from the bloody canvas – only shedding a single tear for the carnage that had been shed on that day.

Other titles coming soon from Lead-Based Books:
Platformed Poison by Adal Smith (2025) (working title)
Human-Like by Adal Smith (TBA)
Doves Fall by Thomas Glover (2025) (working title)